Module 18

By

John Hash

Copyright 2015 by John L. Hash

ISBN 978-0-9831685-1-5

Module 18 is a work of fiction. Any resemblance of any character to a person living or dead is coincidental and not intended.

Other books by John Hash:

Honey Branches: The Meade Estate

Starkeeper

Lero's Mission

Go Get Nadja

Flight to Oblivion

Falcon Strike

This book is dedicated to America and all the good things she stands for.

Prologue

You have walked into an episode in the lives of a group of people you have not met before.

About two years ago, Lero (his nom de guerre) was assigned to a special unit at Davis Monthan Air Force Base in Tucson, Arizona, as a contractor and met Jean there at a church bible study meeting.

Lero is a former airline pilot who took early retirement when his airline failed ten years ago. Since then, he had been rebuilding jet engines for a large airline based in Western Pennsylvania. Lero had been a widower for three years and Jean had been single for several years after a short marriage in her twenties. She is an avionics technician and a college graduate. She came to Tucson with her father and worked for him in his avionics shop until he retired. He died four years ago. She became a member of Jefe's unit when she reconditioned the radios in the Vulcan bomber that was used in the strike on the underground centrifuge enrichment facility near Natanz, Iran. Since then, she has headed the electronic intelligence laboratory and shop for the unit. It was she who designed and built the scanner that intercepted the transmissions regarding the visit of the Grand Ayatollah to Bushehr that enable the team to "paint" his vehicle so the Mirage fighter could hit it. Jean accompanied Lero on the last mission into Disneyland, using the cover that she was his Algerian mistress, while he pretended to be a French avionics technician. Lero was badly hurt when the explosion tore off the front of the hotel from which he was "painting" the target vehicle. Jean and Jefe succeeded in getting an air ambulance into the Bushehr airport to evacuate Lero.

Lero and Jean were both the kind of people who are content to spend time alone, but when they met each other, after years of being alone, they were strongly drawn to each other. As this episode takes place, they have lived together for about a year and a half.

They both worked for Jefe who ran a special unit of contractors at Davis Monthan Air Force Base in Tucson, Arizona. Jefe reported directly to President Thompson, whose nom de guerre is "Mr. Murfree."

(Lero's traveling cover name is Dan Roman. For those inclined to remember aviation trivia, Dan Roman was the co-pilot in the movie "The High and Mighty," played by John Wayne. Lero's "nom de guerre" which each operator has, was chosen by him at the beginning of his first "operation." It is the last syllable of the word "Pistolero" which he chose because his hobby is building and shooting target pistols. Only people who are "associated" would know that.)

When Jefe told the President that he wanted to ease into retirement, the President asked Lero to take over command of the unit. Jefe still consults and helps out with his vast knowledge of people in interesting positions and places and the tradecraft of international special operations. He is an excellent organizer and Lero looks to him for help and advice regularly. They enjoy working with each other.

Lero still has the scars of surgery on his right foreleg. Both bones were broken when an explosion blew off the front of the hotel where he was participating in a mission. The scars are still not quite red, but not quite pink, either. His broken ribs have healed well enough that he does not spasm when Jean hugs him, nor when she rolls over on him in the night. At any time, he can close his eyes and see her in his mind's eye. He thinks she is so beautiful and the sweetest thing that had ever happened to him. He prays every day to thank the Lord for sending her into his life and him into her life.

To be really current with all the parties and their history together, it would be advisable to read "Lero's Mission," then "Go Get Nadja," then "Flight to Oblivion," then "Falcon Strike," all by the same author.

Welcome.

Chapter 1

They were about half way through a bowl of popcorn. Jean was leaning against Lero on the sofa like she loved to do and he loved for her to do. He loved having her warmth next to him. She was wearing the silver satin gown they both liked so much. He was in a Hawaiian shirt and Bermuda shorts. They were watching Megan Kelly on a warm desert night. The inside temperature was comfortable, but it was still over ninety outside.

The lights of a vehicle illuminated the curtain behind them. They heard the crunching sound of wheels in the gravel of the driveway. Lero instinctively reached for their favorite house gun, his well-worn Model 15 Smith and Wesson. Jean pulled back from him and stood, then briskly walked through the kitchen to the bedroom, to get a robe.

It would not have been possible for an observer to have seen through the front curtains, but the lights of the vehicle played on it clearly enough that Lero could tell that the vehicle had turned into their driveway and was sitting there with the lights still on.

As Lero stood and moved over about six feet from the door, a knock came. Not a hard "police" knock, nor the soft knock of a lover sneaking to your door in the night, but a nice moderate knock. Three knocks. Knock, knock, knock. Lero looked toward the kitchen to make sure Jean was safe. She peered around the corner of the stucco opening, tying the sash of her silk kimono.

He went to the door and looked through the peep hole. A man in a blue blazer, white shirt and khakis stood back about five feet from the door.

Lero cracked open the door and spoke to the man. "Yes, can I help you?"

The man held up a leather Federal ID wallet and said, "Secret Service, Mr. Roman. Sorry to disturb you tonight, sir, but Mr. Murfree wants to know if he can speak with you. He would like to come in if that is alright."

"Of course," said Lero. "Give me a moment, please. I am armed and I want to put the weapon away and tell Jean about this."

"It is the President. He wants to come in and visit."

He closed the door. Jean's eyes were as big as saucers.

"I am glad the place is cleaned up. Put the popcorn away and I'll get dressed," she said.

Lero put his revolver in its safety place and again opened the door.

"Sir, I need to do a brief security search before he comes in. Is that OK," asked the Secret Service agent.

"Give us a moment, officer, and you may certainly come in. Just a moment."

He closed the door just as Jean appeared in a dark gray pin striped pants suit, heels and a blouse like she was going to a meeting at the base.

"He needs to do a brief security search," said Lero to Jean.

"Okay," she said. "Let him in."

Lero opened the door again and invited the officer in.

He smiled and asked, "Are you the only persons in the house?"

Jean said, "Yes."

He asked, "Ma'am, is it alright if I look around a bit?"

(The house is owned by Jean and the courtesy was extended to her as the owner.)

She smiled and said: "Sure."

He smiled again and set out through the kitchen. In thirty seconds, he returned and said, "Thank you for your courtesy. Mr. Murfree wants to visit with you both alone. I will be on the porch if I am needed. I will turn off the outside light. Another officer is in the car."

By this time, the lights on the vehicle had been turned off and the motor, too.

As Lero and Jean stood in their living room, President Thompson opened the door and came in. He immediately hugged Lero and Jean and told them how glad he was to see them. Jean asked if he would like a drink. He asked if he and Lero could share an O'Douls. Jean smiled and went to the refrigerator to get them.

(Neither the President nor Lero drink alcohol. O'Doul's alcohol free beer is a favorite of theirs.)

Lero asked the President to sit, but the President said he would rather stand for a few minutes.

The President said, "I get the reports of your recovery, but I wanted to stop and see you and see for myself how you are doing."

"I am healing up pretty well, sir. The doctors have given me first class care."

"Dan, you and Jean are so valuable to me, as contractors and as friends. I just wanted to visit a bit to tell you how grateful we are for what you do and have done."

"It is an honor to serve," said Lero. "We enjoy it thoroughly."

"Janice gave me strict instructions to say 'hello' and to tell you both how grateful she is, too."

"You are treasured friends," said Jean.

By now, the President was ready to sit. He clinked his bottle of O'Douls with Lero's and sat in the large chair opposite the sofa.

Over the next few moments, the President grew serious, and holding his bottle of O'Douls in front of him at the table, he looked at it and then looked up at them. He said: "As you know, I have many sources of information, some official and some un-official. Sometimes we can act in the open, with our regular forces, but sometimes, we need to act quicker and with more secrecy than would be possible with our regular forces."

"The elves in Disneyland have, for some time, as you know, been preparing to produce an atomic weapon. At the same time, their rhetoric has been quite heated. I feel that we must take both very seriously. To ignore these obvious signs is a luxury we cannot afford. The clowns in the Congress are quite divided about what, if anything, to do about the continued threat. Their grandstanding and posturing is a continuous source of nausea for all of us who must observe them."

"I chose to drop in on you both like this to share something with you that I want to be kept very close. That is the reason I instructed my Secret Service detail to wait outside. For now, we three are the only ones who will share what I am about to tell you."

"As you know, the elves in Disneyland have strategically dispersed their facilities and buried several of them under considerable earth and rock and cement cover and some have been placed in mines and caves. The mission with the Vulcan bomber, while quite successful, only resulted in a delay of their progress of about nine months. They got right back at it and have made amazing strides since then."

"One of the most important things that Nadja was able to tell us is the purpose of some of the various facilities that they have. The isotopes are being produced at Adak and Natanz, we know. The weaponizing of the resulting isotopes is probably being done at Qom. But what we have not been able to find out is where they are working on and assembling the trigger to set off a device. Just two days ago, we received credible information from a secret informant about which facility is building the trigger. As you both know, it was determined by the early scientists that two masses of fissionable material must be brought together at very high speed to cause the reaction that we regard as a nuclear explosion. The bomb at Trinity, south of Albuquerque, used small charges of high explosives set in a spherical array, all detonated at the same time to achieve the first atomic blast. It was an awesome sight for the observers who were in a concrete bunker only ten thousand yards from the tower where the device was detonated."

"But, I digress. With a high level of confidence, we believe that the elves are just now assembling a trigger which will achieve a nuclear blast. Our information is that they intend to transport the trigger to the isotope facility, load the nuclear materials and then transport the device to another site for an underground test."

"As you also both know, I get a daily briefing from the Intelligence Community. Nothing has appeared in it about this situation. Either our intel guys don't know about this or they are strategically withholding it from me, possibly for political reasons.

"I want you two to head a team to intercept the trigger before it gets to the isotope facility or test facility and destroy or disable it. Later, we will follow up with a strike on the facility that produced the trigger to further set the elves back, but we need to stop this test first."

"Do either of you know of any reason why you cannot undertake this task for me?"

He studied them as they digested what they had just heard and while they thought about what the President had just said. Then Jean looked at Lero and they locked eyes for a moment. Then Jean said, "Sir, we have no impediments. We will give it our best effort."

Lero nodded his agreement.

"Good. Please give me an update daily, if you can, by scrambled telephone or coded message by satellite phone. I will make any personnel or material available to help you. We need to be ready quickly and then we will stand by for the signal that the hen is on the nest when they intend to begin the transport. I will give you particulars later, but my source will dial a particular number by cell phone to give me the signal. The call is not to be answered. The call itself is the signal that the transport is under way. Any details I learn about the transport I will tell you immediately."

The President paused to take a swig of O'Douls.

Jean asked: "Have you eaten recently. Would you like something?"

"No, thanks," said the President. "I need to get going. Thanks for seeing me on such short notice. Thank you for helping me."

With that, he slapped his knees and rose to his feet. Lero and Jean got to their feet, too. The President hugged Jean and shook hands with Lero.

Then he said: "This is scary business. I am glad I have you two to rely on."

"We are honored you chose us," said Lero and moved so the President could get to the door. In a moment, he was gone. They watched through the cracked door as he got into the Suburban with his two security men. The lights came on and the Suburban slowly backed out of the driveway. In a moment, they were gone.

Lero and Jean looked at each other. It was a long look.

"Do you want to finish the bowl of popcorn and watch the news for a while?" she asked.

"No," he whispered. "I would rather watch you take off that pants suit and walk toward me."

She smiled sweetly and turned toward the back of the house.

Chapter 2

Jean was at work at her shop in the late morning when the telephone rang. After she said "hello," the voice on the other end simply said, "Hold please for Mr. Murfree." She waited for about twenty seconds before she heard the familiar voice.

"Say the word, please," the voice said. Jean hesitated just a moment and then said "Durango." Now the President and Jean each knew that they were indeed talking to the person intended.

"Good morning. How are things going?" asked the President.

"Fine, sir. Right now we are busy mapping and measuring distances and checking road and railroad types between the known facilities. Are there any clues about timing yet?" she asked.

"Things continue to be closely monitored. We expect to hear something in the next week or so. Could you and Lero meet with me at the house at Vail this Saturday? I managed to acquire Gerald Ford's former house and it is a nice place for me and Janice to hide out once in a while," he said.

"I am sure we can come, sir. What time on Saturday would you want to meet?"

"Let's plan on a late morning meeting. I will need about an hour with you both."

"Fine, we will see you then," she said.

"Thanks. You will receive codes and passwords by scrambler the day before. See you then."

She started to say "Goodbye," but the line went dead.

Chapter 3

When Lero picked her up for lunch, she had a chance to tell him about the call as they sat in the Grand Cherokee at the Sonic drive in. They appreciated the tinted windows for the privacy and it helped with the temperature, too.

"Mr. Murfree called about an hour ago," she said. "He wants to meet with us at Vail on Saturday late in the morning. Can we do that?"

"Of course," said Lero. "We just need to decide how to go up there. If the weather looks good, we can take the Twin Comanche. If it is not so good, we can fly commercial."

"I have never been to Vail before," she said. "Could we stay overnight and look around a bit?"

"Fine with me if the meeting with Mr. Murfree does not cause us to cut our time short. I have never been to Vail before, either. I'll check the weather to see if we can fly ourselves and why don't you check on seat availability on commercial flights."

"Okay," she said and popped another French fry into her mouth.

Later, he returned to his office. Now it was his office. It had been Jefe's office for several years and now that Jefe was officially retired, but actually only phasing out over a period of months, Lero had moved into the director's office in the Quonset hut on the east boundary road at Davis Monthan Air Force Base. Out the front window of the waiting room, which was coated to prevent inward visibility, they could look out over the vast fields of mothballed aircraft. Just across the road from them was a field of B-52s. The jet engines, if still on the aircraft, had plastic covers in the intakes and exhausts. The windows of the flight decks were covered with a spray-on plastic cover that could be removed with a particular solvent when necessary.

Lero's office was rather Spartan. One desk near the back wall, a large leather sofa opposite, and two leather chairs on either side. There was a nice mahogany conference table near the opposite wall, with six nice wood captain's chairs around it. His personal computer was a laptop on the top of the desk. He awakened it and when it had booted, he keyed in the code to tap into DUATS, the FAA sponsored flight planning software for pilots. He typed in his account name and his password. Then, he chose the weather facility and keyed in the date of his flight and the departure and destination identifiers for the airports where he would take off and land. In way less time than it takes to describe it, the screen filled with digits and symbols that he could read to see what the forecast weather was for the route of flight. Generally, the weather was good, with light winds aloft forecast for the area. Since he and Jean planned to stick around Vail for a day or so, he did not check the forecast weather for the planned return trip. He knew that he could check DUATS again in Vail on his laptop and get a briefing when they thought about returning.

He dropped out of the weather feature and went to flight planning. He keyed in DM, the FAA identifier for Davis Monthan Air Force Base and the ID for Vail, Eagle County, Colorado, EKE. He chose to plan a flight from VOR to VOR, even though their Twin Comanche had a GPS receiver.

(Note: VOR meant vertical omnidirectional ranging, a technical term to describe these navigation radios which are dispersed around the country. There are approximately one thousand of them and they broadcast three hundred sixty one signals constantly which enables a radio receiver in the aircraft to determine the direction to or from the VOR. The United States has many, many

VOR low altitude routes and high altitude routes, also known a Jet Routes that act as highways in the sky to organize air traffic and make air travel more exact and safe.)

The software quickly displayed the route from Tucson to Eagle County. The list of identifiers of the VORs were displayed in a vertical list, with the departure airport at the bottom and the destination at the top. Frequencies of them were displayed, as well as altitude above sea level, the distance from one to the next and the magnetic heading from each to the next.

Lero keyed the computer to give a print order to the printer in the outer office. With quick efficiency, Velma, the office manager brought it in.

Lero got out his Sectional charts for the route and his Low Altitude Enroute charts for the same route. He noticed that the trip he had chosen to map out was for four hundred ninety eight and a half nautical miles and an estimated time enroute of three hours and fifty minutes at the proposed ground speed of one hundred thirty knots. This was a conservative speed which the Twin Comanche could easily exceed, but he wanted to be cautious in case of a change in the winds aloft. The winds aloft for the route of flight were printed on the lower part of the page from the printer. Airports in the vicinity of the route had forecast winds aloft generally coming from two five zero degrees and varied from five to fifteen knots at an altitude of three to six thousand feet above ground level. That was the report of current winds aloft. He would need to get the forecast winds aloft before takeoff to make sure the trip was safe and feasible.

He spread the Sectional charts on the conference table. As a precaution, he checked the position of the airports close to the proposed line of flight for runway lengths and height above sea level. As an easterner, he was always impressed with the height above sea level of the terrain and the airports in the west. Davis Monthan Airport was at two thousand seven hundred four feet above mean sea level and Eagle County was six thousand five hundred forty seven feet. Each had plenty of runway length for their Twin Comanche, but he realized that the airplane would be producing power and lift as if it were already flying at four thousand feet even though it was still on the runway at Davis Monthan. However, with only him and Jean aboard, plus luggage and a full load of fuel, they would still be over four hundred pounds below maximum gross weight.

The VORs for the route of flight were Tucson, Zuni, about one hundred ninety three nautical miles to the north east, then Gallup, New Mexico, Cortex, Grand Junction, Rifle and Grand Junction, Colorado and then Snow VOR just before Eagle County near Vail. With all this information, he folded up the charts and the DUATS information and put them in his briefcase to take home to review with Jean.

Chapter 4

Next, he dialed the satellite phone number for Jefe. After the usual preliminary noises, it made the sound for ringing on the other end. After four rings, Jefe answered.

"Hello."

"This is Lero, say the word."

Jefe said "'Sedona.' What is the good word today?"

Lero said: "Houston."

Now they both knew they were indeed talking to the person intended.

"How are you and Alita doing these days?" asked Lero.

"Fine," said Jefe. "We had a fish dinner in town last night on the wharf that was unforgettable. You and Jean must come visit us here sometime soon."

"We would love to. Maybe later this summer," said Lero.

"Is something up?" asked Jefe.

"Not just now, but I may need some assistance in the next couple of weeks. What are your plans for the next couple of weeks?"

"We planned to stay here for the next three weeks at least. No need to be anywhere else just now and we enjoy the sunlight and the pool so much. Will you require me to travel any," asked Jefe.

"We have been invited to a costume party in Disneyland, but the dates are not certain just yet. I think I will need you to help arrange our transport in your vicinity and the transport of other invited guests," said Lero.

"Thanks for the heads up. I will keep a bag semi-packed and will be ready to help whenever you need me. Is everything doing okay otherwise?"

"Yes, Jean said to tell you both hello and she hopes we can get to see you soon. Velma has the office running smoothly."

"Well, thanks again for the heads-up. Let me know if I can do anything," said Jefe.

"Will do, and thanks," said Lero. "Bye."

"Bye."

As he walked up, Alita asked him who called.

"It was Lero. He wanted to consult a bit."

"Does he need you to help him?"

"Yes, but we probably will not need to leave here to do so."

"That's great. It is heavenly here. The weather is marvelous and this pool is superb. By the way, you simply must get more sun, dear. Get out of those restrictive clothes and put some lotion on me, please."

Jefe smiled broadly as he started to unbutton his shirt.

Chapter 5

Lero finished up his other work and left the office when Velma left, about ten after six. He drove to the west side of the base and exited through the secure gate. The guards recognized him and waved him through. In a couple of minutes, he pulled up in the driveway of 123 Sunset Lane, Jean's home that he had shared with her for about eighteen months now.

He took his brief case in with him, as usual. Jean had already arrived and was in the living room when he came in. They met each other in the middle of the living room and shared a moment of affection. She felt so wonderful against him. He closed his eyes and said a prayer of thanksgiving.

"What would you like for dinner?" she asked.

"Something easy for you to fix while I help," he said.

"If you will make a bowl of salad, I will fix us spaghetti and meat balls," she said.

"Fine, I'm in," he said as he walked to the bedroom to change out of his day clothes.

By the time he returned to the kitchen, she had a large copper kettle on the stove heating and a smaller sauce pan with sauce and meat balls in it heating slowly on the stove. He walked up behind her and she turned to him as he did. He reached around her waist and pulled her to him and gave her a big kiss on the neck. The casual observer might conclude that this was extraordinary behavior on their part, but is was perfectly normal for them.

He built a large bowl of tossed salad and toasted some garlic bread while she cooked the pasta and sauce. It all came together nicely and he made a cruet of his homemade wine vinegar and olive oil salad dressing. They filled bowls, plates and glasses and sat to eat at the kitchen table which was small enough that they could easily reach across it to touch each other's arms and hands.

Between bites, he said, "I talked to Jefe today. He and Alita are on Keros at their place. I needed to alert him and her that we may need their services in the next three or four weeks. They are enthused to help us, even though they don't know any details."

"Alita told me that they are very fond of sunbathing in the altogether there, next to their pool and that the Grecian sunshine is intoxicating," Jean shared.

"If we visit them, they will probably dress more conventionally," said Lero, "but I would love to see their place. He said the seafood is wonderful in town."

There was not any left-over spaghetti, but there was some salad left over, so he put it in a container and put it in the refrigerator. With the dishes in the dishwasher, they adjourned to the living room.

He said, "I brought some charts home so we can plan our trip to Vail. When you are ready, I can review them with you."

"I am so excited to get to go to Vail, and to fly cross country to get there is an extra treat," she said.

(Note: Lero is a retired airline transport pilot and worked for several years after the Air Force for an airline that ultimately failed. He took retirement and moved to western Pennsylvania and overhauled jet engines for a large airline for several years before he got involved in this line of work and met Jean. Jean is a freshly minted Private Pilot. She has worked at Davis Monthan for many years, both with her father and after his death. She is an avionics technician and is "attached" to the unit.)

"I brought a WAC chart (World Aeronautical Chart) so we could plan the trip," said Lero. I used the DUATS service to gather some basic information, but I thought it would be good training for you to plan the trip with me."

(Note: DUATS is the Direct User Access Terminal service of the FAA to allow pilots to obtain weather briefings and plan flights using information from the FAA computer.)

"Sure, where do we start?" asked Jean.

"I am so glad you got your Private ticket. We can enjoy the plane so much more now that you are a pilot. I feel safer with you being a pilot, both for my and for your sake."

"I have worked on aircraft radios for years and always thought somehow I would take flight training, but living with you and seeing how much you love it, pushed me over the edge. I am so grateful to have gotten my training here on the base. Where to we start?"

Lero unfolded the Chart and spread it on the table next to the west wall. She sat adjacent to him (ninety degrees away) and they started the planning procedure.

Note to the technically curious: If you would like to see a chart like Lero is using, key in SkyVector.com on your browser and you can not only see what Jean and Lero are looking at, but follow along as they travel to Vail.

"Well, we know that the destination in Vail, Colorado and the departure airport is Davis Monthan. Basically the course line is north northeasterly. Davis Monthan is at twenty seven hundred four feet above sea level and Eagle County, where we intend to land, is at six thousand five hundred forty seven feet. This will be a trip of about five hundred miles. I thought it best to deviate from the straight line between the two airports to avoid high terrain and keep us over a series of navigation radios and airports where we can land if we need to."

He knew that Jean with her experience as an expert avionics technician knew as much as anybody about VORs.

"I thought we would go first to Zuni VOR, then on up to Gallup, New Mexico, here, as he pointed. Then northerly to Junction City, Colorado, where we would turn easterly and fly to Rifle VOR at Rifle, Colorado and then up the valley to Snow VOR just west of Eagle County Airport. The flight planning software gave me all the vectors and distances and times, assuming we average one hundred thirty knots, but I intend to use the GPS to cross check the course." he said.

"Don't we expect to average faster than that?" asked Jean.

"Yes, but I like to build in a little tolerance in case the winds aloft shift on us from the forecast direction and intensity. Another thing is that we will have to pass through a couple of Military Operations Areas. These are controlled by Albuquerque Center and we will have to call Flight Service or Albuquerque to find out it they are being used in the area we intend to pass through. One is Jackal MOA and the other is Outlaw MOA."

"I remember this from the Private Pilot written and our lessons. What are the altitudes of the MOAs that we will pass through?" she asked.

"Jackal goes from six thousand MSL to forty thousand feet. Outlaw is from the surface to fifty thousand feet."

"I'm glad you would rather avoid the high terrain. Will it add a lot of time to our trip?"

"About forty miles and thirteen minutes. I think it is well worth it," said Lero.

"Me too," she said. "That peak there just east of the course line is over twelve thousand feet. What altitude do you think we will use?"

"Well, east bound, we need to choose odd thousand feet plus five hundred to abide by Visual Flight Rules. I think nine thousand five hundred will be good."

"Does our Comanche have enough fuel to get us there without a fuel stop?" she asked.

"Yes, we have ninety gallons of fuel capacity in four tanks. Preliminarily, it looks like we will use about sixty five gallons. That leaves us a nice reserve."

"Since Mr. Murfree wants to meet with us in the early afternoon on Friday, we can leave here about eight AM and make it in good time.

"I think this is exciting. Our first cross country together. Terrific," she said.

Chapter 6

The next afternoon, Lero called the Flight Service Station and asked for a weather briefing for their intended route of flight. The winds aloft forecast was especially important. The forecast for six thousand feet above ground level was for mild to moderate winds, approximately twenty knots, from two four zero degrees, with minimal turbulence. This was a left quartering tail wind relative to most of their flight path and was good news.

Lero telephoned Jean and told her the weather was good for a visual flight rules flight to Vail the next morning. They finished their separate days of work and looked forward to the final preparations to go to Vail.

In addition to their luggage with clothing and overnight gear, Lero had prepared his leather satchel that the pilots called the "brain bag," which he had filled with all of the intended and potential flight charts that they might need. He checked the batteries in the portable intercom system and closed the case with its snaps.

November seven seven seven niner Papa waited patiently for them in its hangar on the base. It had mid time engines and props, recent oil changes, and a fresh battery. It would be fueled in the morning as they departed.

Jean wanted to go over the chart that Lero had marked with the route of flight. The flight path went north east for about two hundred ten miles then turned almost due north for another two hundred miles, then turned north eastward again from Grand Junction to Eagle County Airport. She carefully folded the chart and put it in her bag, so they could refer to it before and during the flight.

Lero had a spread sheet with information on all the VORs and airports on or near the flight path that he gave her to put with the chart.

They awakened at six just before the alarm went off. It was still dark, but there was a brightening lighter blue in the eastern sky. By the time they showered and dressed, the sun was clearly about to dawn. Lero had cautioned Jean that they should eat a light breakfast, so they did and checked the house one last time and went out the door with their bags.

Sure enough, Seven niner Papa was waiting for them in its hangar. They pulled it out into the morning light and checked it over. They checked the oil in each engine, drained some fuel from the bottom of each fuel tank to make sure any accumulated water was discarded, then they boarded, started and taxied to the fixed base operator to get the fuel topped up.

Once that was done, Lero got up on the right wing on the boarding pad and offered Jean a hand up. She held onto the door while he got in first since he would be in the left seat. Then, she swung in. They organized themselves, fastened seat and shoulder belts, plugged in and arranged the intercom headsets and checked them by powering them up. Once that was done, Lero flipped the master switch up and tuned the communications radio to the Clearance Delivery frequency.

"Davis Monthan Clearance, Twin Comanche Seven seven seven niner Papa requesting clearance on VFR flight plan to Eagle County, Colorado, as filed."

"Comanche seven seven seven niner papa, VFR flight plan approved as filed, squawk four one four one after departure, fly runway heading, contact departure on one one niner decimal seven on departure. Contact ground on point niner."

"Thank you, clearance, seven niner pop over to ground."

Next Lero tuned in the Automatic Terminal Information Service for a recorded message with local current and forecast weather and any notices to airmen about any facility or radio that might be off the air for repairs.

"Davis Monthan Information Sierra. Sky clear, Visibility ten or greater. No ceiling. Wind fifteen knots from two five zero degrees. Temperature is five. Barometric pressure is two niner niner seven. Report on first contact that you have Information Sierra."

Lero set the barometric pressure on the altimeter and it read within twenty feet of airport elevation.

Next he called Ground Control.

"Davis Monthan ground, Comanche seven seven seven niner papa at the Fixed Base Operator, ready to taxi to the active, with Sierra."

"Comanche niner papa, taxi to runway three zero, hold short of landing traffic."

"Roger, niner papa to Runway three zero, will hold short."

Lero and Jean left the door ajar and he began the drill to start the engines. Mixture was pushed up to full rich, the electric fuel pump was turned on long enough to see pressure on the fuel flow gauge, then he opened the little window to his left in the side window and said: "Clear" to warn anyone in the vicinity that he was about to start an engine. He gave a quick look around and then pushed the starter switch for the left engine. It turned over a couple of times, then fired and settled into a smooth idle. He repeated the procedure for the right engine and once it was going, he reached over across Jean and pulled the door shut and latched it. Then he released the brakes and they taxied slowly out of the fixed base operator's area onto the taxiway to the east end of the active runway, about a quarter of a mile to the north.

When they got to the western threshold of Runway three zero, so named because it lay within five degrees of three hundred degrees magnetic, he pulled over onto what is call the run up area. Now, he took out the pre-flight check list and read each item aloud so he and Jean could double check each item.

"Okay, fuel on proper tanks, door locked and latched, electric fuel pumps on, flaps set, now we will run up the engines to check the magnetos." He pushed the throttle for the left engine forward a bit and the engine revved up. Then he turned off each of the two magnetos in turn to check each of them for proper operation. He repeated this for the right engine.

"Okay, he said, let's call the tower."

He looked over at her and asked if she were ready to go.

She asked: "Did you check everything?" He said "Yes," and gave her a little kiss on the lips, to complete their pre-flight ritual.

"Davis Monthan Tower, Comanche seven seven seven niner papa is ready to go on Runway three zero, holding short."

"Comanche niner papa, inbound traffic has cleared the runway, you are cleared for take off, Runway three zero."

"Roger, niner papa is rolling," said Lero and advanced the throttles to taxi onto the active runway. Once established on the center line, he slowly advanced the throttles to their stops and the sleek Comanche began to eat up the runway.

After a take-off run of about a thousand feet, they lifted into the morning sky. Once Lero concluded that they would not need to return to the runway, he flipped the gear switch up and the electric landing gear began to retract. They could feel the additional acceleration as the drag of the landing gear diminished.

As they passed through five hundred feet above the runway elevation, the tower called and instructed him to contact Departure.

"Departure, niner papa off of Runway one two, squawking four zero four zero."

"Comanche seven niner papa, radar contact,right turn to course approved, climb and maintain six thousand feet, report reaching."

"Departure, niner papa, roger, left to course, up to six thousand, will report reaching." The Comanche began a slow turn to a northerly heading as it continued to climb into the morning sun.

Lero turned to a heading of three six zero degrees and tuned in the Tucson VOR. He continued to guide the Twin Comanche north until it was fifteen degrees from the Tucson VOR, then he turned right to a heading of fifteen degrees. During the first ten minutes of the flight, after Departure instructed them to do so, they climbed to nine thousand five hundred feet and leveled off.

"Tucson Approach, Comanche seven seven seven niner Papa is level at niner thousand five hundred. Requests flight following if you have the time."

"Seven niner papa, radar contact, we show you level at niner thousand five hundred. Say destination, please, and route of flight."

"Seven niner papa is going to Eagle County, Colorado by way of Zuni VOR and Grand Junction VOR."

"Roger, seven niner papa, contact Phoenix Approach now on one two six decimal six. Good day."

"Roger, Tucson Approach, thanks, seven niner papa.

Lero turned the dial of the communications radio to one two six decimal six and called:
Phoenix Approach: "Phoenix Approach, Comanche seven seven seven niner papa, with you, level at niner thousand five hundred, squawking four one four one."

"Roger, seven niner papa, radar contact."

Now, they were really on their way, flying outbound from the area of coverage of Phoenix Approach, and soon to be handed off to Phoenix Center for the bulk of the trip. Jean looked over at Lero. With his dark aviator glasses and his David Clark headset, his profile broadcast the image of a man truly in his element. He looked like the bomber pilot he had been trained to be. She knew that he was comfortable in the air and belonged up here. The most important thing she thought as she watched him aviate was she was so grateful that he loved her so much.

He noticed her turn her head toward him and he turned to look at her.

"Beautiful day, isn't it?" he asked.

"Yes, indeed," she said into the mike of the headset she wore. It was so nice to be able to converse in a normal tone, even whisper if needed, and she was thankful for the intercom and the headsets.

"Will we go to the left of that mountain ahead?" she asked.

"Yes, our course line will take us to the west of it. The perspective is kind like a moving carpet isn't it?"

"Yes," she said. "I never get over how beautiful it is up here."

"Lindbergh said that aviation reveals the true face of the earth. Quite a mouthful."

"Yes," she said. "It is so beautiful. How far to Zuni VOR?"

"One hundred six nautical miles. The GPS shows us about two miles west of the straight line between Tucson and Zuni, in good shape. I put Zuni in as a waypoint in the GPS, so it could cross check the Navigation radio. At

Zuni, we will turn to almost north for most of the trip. That will take us west of the highest peaks and won't add but a few minutes to the trip."

"Seven niner papa, contact Denver center now on one two seven decimal two five."

"Roger, Phoenix, over to Denver on one two seven decimal two five."

"Good morning, Denver Center, Comanche seven seven seven niner papa is with you at niner thousand five hundred, squawking four one four one."

After a pause, Lero and Jean heard: "Comanche seven niner papa, Denver Center, radar contact, squawk two two five four for us please."

"Comanche seven niner papa, radar contact, radar readout indicates niner thousand five hundred."

"Seven niner papa, roger, thanks."

"Let's switch to the outboard tanks now and fly them for a while. I would rather land using the main tanks and we can come back to them once we use up most of the fuel in the outboard tanks."

She watched as he switched the left engine to the outboard and then the right engine. No dip in the fuel pressure indicators, so all was well.

Out the windscreen, Jean spotted the Zuni VOR nestled in the foothills of north eastern Arizona.

"There is Zuni," she said.

"The GPS shows eight nautical miles. We will make a course correction to the north after we pass over."

Lero adjusted the heading indicator and watched the Zuni VOR pass under the nose.

As the navigation radio window changed from "TO" to "FROM," Lero banked a bit to the left and brought the plane to a heading of three five five.

"Why don't you take it for a while?" he asked.

"Oh, I would love to," said Jean. "My first twin time."

He gave her the heading numbers and watched as she put her hands on the yoke. As soon as she had done that, he took his hand off of his yoke. With the revolutions set at twenty four hundred and the manifold pressure at twenty four inches, the Twin Comanche hummed along contentedly. A nice smooth morning. Lero noticed that the quartering tail wind was adding about twenty knots to their ground speed. That would reduce the planned time of the trip by about half an hour if it remained consistent, he thought.

Jean had hunched up a bit after she took the yoke and was obviously trying hard to hold heading.

"Relax a bit. If you fly the whole trip that tense, you will be exhausted when we get there. Let the bird fly. Just nudge it once in a while and relax."

She smiled at him and sat back in the seat a bit.

"I just want to please you with my flying," she said.

"You please me all the time," he said. "Just relax and enjoy the view."

"Twin Comanche seven niner papa, you have fighter jet traffic at your eight o'clock northbound, should pass well clear, but advise them in sight."

Lero and Jean looked to the left behind the wing. After looking for a few seconds, the spotted the fighters, slightly above them and moving swiftly northward.

"Beautiful sight, a pair of F-16s out for a little practice," said Lero and keyed his mike.

"Denver center, seven niner papa has the traffic, well clear, thanks."

"Seven niner papa, roger, Denver Center."

They made the course turn at Grand Junction and aimed the plane up a long valley in the mountain range toward Vail.

"Denver Center, Seven niner papa would like to begin our descent for Eagle County now."

"That is approved, seven niner papa, have a good day and contact Eagle County Unicom for advisories."

Lero dialed the communication radio to the Unicom frequency for Eagle County, and listened. No other broadcasts interrupted the silence.

He keyed the mike. "Eagle County Unicom, Eagle County unicom, November seven seven seven niner papa is over Grand Junction, landing Eagle County, requesting advisories."

After a pause of about ten seconds, a lady's voice came over the Unicom.

"Seven niner papa, roger, Eagle County altimeter setting is two niner niner five. No reported traffic, but commercial flight is expected in about twenty minutes from the east. Report passing over Snow VOR inbound, please."

"Niner papa, thanks, will report Snow inbound, level at niner thousand five hundred now."

The elevation of the terrain below had changed considerably since they left Tucson. The altitude of the ground below was over six thousand feet and gradually rising as they flew east up the valley toward Vail. Massive mountains on both sides of the valley seemed to be guarding the entrance to the valley.

As the GPS indicated five miles to the Snow VOR, Jean spotted the Eagle County airport, with its runway lying parallel to the interstate highway below.

"There it is," she said into the mike on her headset.

"Oh, good," said Lero. "Is that it to the right of the road ahead?"

"Yes, it looks a little to the right of the road, but parallel to it."

"Yes, I've got it," said Lero and keyed his mike.

"Eagle County, Seven niner papa has Eagle Count in sight. Entering the pattern right downwind for runway eight."

"Seven niner papa, continue to Eagle County. No other reported traffic."

"Roger, Eagle County. Seven niner papa."

Lero had pulled the throttles back to sixteen inches of manifold pressure and the Twin Comanche slowed as he maintained altitude. When the airspeed dropped below one hundred fifty miles per hour, he tripped the landing gear switch and the gear started down. The yellow light on the panel went out as the motor pushed the gear out. When it was down and locked, a green light came on below the yellow light.

"Gear down and locked," Lero said into the mike. As the airspeed bled off to one hundred twenty five miles per hour, he put the flaps down halfway. The plane slowed again and he began a gradual descent to the left of the runway on the downwind leg of his approach.

"Eagle County, niner papa is turning right base for runway two niner at Eagle County," he said into the mike. No one replied.

He turned the plane to the right about a half mile past the western end of the runway below to the right. As they turned perpendicular to the runway, Lero looked to the left and right to see if there were any other planes in sight. There were none and he prepared to turn right again to line up on final approach. Now they would be into the wind and the ground speed would decrease. Airspeed was the important thing, though, and he maintained one twenty on the approach. Altitude was now seven thousand nine hundred and decreasing at about eight hundred feet a minute.

"Eagle County Unicom, Southwest Flight Six five five, a Boeing Seven thirty seven, about forty east of the field, requesting advisories."

'Southwest six five five, Eagle County, altimeter setting is two niner niner five, Comanche traffic turning final for runway two niner, no other reported traffic."

Now Lero and Jean were lined up on final for Runday two niner at Eagle County.

"Eagle County traffic, Comanche niner papa is final for runway two niner at Eagle County," said Lero into his headset. He bled the airspeed down to one hundred five as they came down final approach. With just a mild gust of wind to disturb them about fifty feet above the runway, seven niner papa settled onto the runway with a chirp of its main gear tires and rolled on the center line. In a bit, Lero turned off the active runway onto the taxiway and broadcast: "Seven niner papa is clear of the active at Eagle County."

They taxied to the fixed base operator's area. A line man was waiting with paddles to guide them to a tie down spot.

"Welcome to Eagle County," he said. "Will you be overnight and will you need fuel?"

"We will be over night and will buy fuel when we depart," said Lero, out the little storm window in his side window.

The line man nodded and Lero reached over and opened the door for Jean.

"How beautiful," she said. "The flight, the airport and everything. Thanks for letting me fly some."

"You can log two hours for today. I thought you did fine." She smiled and kissed him sweetly. Their headset mikes collided as they kissed.

Chapter 7

The lady at the counter in the fixed base welcomed them to Eagle County and said: "Mr. Roman, one of your associates left a car for you to use while you are here. It is the brown Ford Fusion in the lot out back. Here are the keys. If you will call ahead when you are ready to depart, we will fuel you up as you direct. Have a nice visit to Vail. Can I do anything to help?"

"Thank you very much. We are fine for now. May I pull the car out to the plane to unload luggage?"

"Sure thing," she said, "Just pull up to the gate and I will open it for you."

Jean and Lero each adjourned to the respective rest rooms and then went out to the parking lot.

Mr. Murfree had left a map in an envelope on the front seat to guide them to their place.

They gave the town of Vail a good look as they passed through. Plenty of interesting places to visit later.

In twenty minutes, they pulled up to the gate to the right of the road. The numbers in black stood out against the gray native stone gate posts and fencing. 6755.

Lero pulled up to the gate and rolled the window down. He spoke in the direction of the small speaker on the post to his left.

"Lero and Jean to see Mr. Murfree," he said.

Without a reply, the gate swung open and they went in.

The house was out of sight of the gate. The road swung around to the right and the house was set back above the road a bit and nestled in a notch in the mountainside. It gave good security on the back side and a magnificent view of the valley on the front side.

As they pulled up into the parking area, a Secret Service agent stepped over to the car, before they got out.

"Good morning, sir," he said. "Please look into the green light for ten seconds and do not blink." Lero turned slightly and looked into the retina scanner. In ten seconds the officer withdrew the scanner and noted a green LED had lit. He now stepped over to the passenger door and asked Jean to do the same. The same green LED came on after she was scanned.

The agent said, "Welcome to both of you. We will bring your luggage up. Go up the steps to the front porch. Mr. Murfree is expecting you."

"Thank you, officer," said Lero and took Jean's arm to go up the stairs.

Chapter 8

The President and First Lady greeted them warmly and invited them in. He gave them a brief tour of the floor they were on and explained the amenities and features. It was nice for the group to actually see one another again. They chatted warmly about the trip and the subject of Lero's injuries and recovery came up.

"I want to thank you again, sir, for sending that air ambulance to Bushehr. Without the good medical treatment I received, I probably would have lost my right leg. Now, thanks to good rehabilitation and Jean's good cooking, I think I have regained my health."

"I am so glad," said the President. "You both are very special to us, both professionally and personally. Let's have some lunch and you can tell us about your flight."

The dining room table was a massive native oak piece, about eight feet square and the top was made of pieces three inches thick with a nice satin finish.

The first lady had personally supervised the preparation of the lunch: Gazpacho soup to start, thin sliced rare roast beef for sandwiches, mild, but tasty horseradish sauce, and a mountain of salad with several choices of dressings. A steaming chafing dish had thick sliced French bread and there was a compote of melted cheese sauce for dipping.

The First Lady told them how the upper floor was laid out and how much they enjoyed their getaways here. Now that their children were in college, they could travel more, within the strictures of a busy schedule, of course.

After a leisurely lunch, they adjourned to the President's study. They sat around a smaller table, about six feet by eight and found it covered by a leather sheet with various brands from the nearby cattle ranches. The President pulled off the cover to reveal a large map of Iran. There were several red and blue stickers on the map. From his seat, the President said: "First of all, this room is as secure as we can make it. It is swept often and I had it swept again this morning, just to be cautious."

"I have asked Janice to join us for two reasons: First, she has a Top Secret Clearance of her own from the time she served at NSA. That was where we met, by the way. I had been posted with the CIA to Langley and a group of us went up to Fort Meade for a briefing. I have often accused her of using an odorless psychotropic gas in the briefing room or using some kind of tractor beam on me, but I was lost shortly after I saw her for the first time."

They all shared a laugh.

"As you know, Janice's father was the Chief of Naval Operations some years ago and he could have gotten her into any college she and he wanted, but she won an academic scholarship to Emory in Atlanta and graduated there with a degree in Middle East Studies.

"Second, what I am about to discuss with you is so important, that I want someone I trust completely here with me and in Washington that you can rely on once you put your plan into motion, in case you cannot reach me at a critical time. I don't intend to be difficult to reach, but my job is complicated and there are brief periods when no one can reach me quickly. Janice will have full authority to give you permission to energize any phase of the mission."

"The reasons we chose you both for this mission are numerous: You both are pilots, you both are fluent in Farsi, French and Arabic. You have the skills sets we need in other areas. Avionics, telemetry, electronic communications and computer technology. You have both been to Disneyland before and are familiar with the territory, you both are familiar and skilled with 'military hardware,' and, most of all, we trust you completely."

By now, Jean and Lero were sitting upright near the front edge of their chairs. The map before them covered the whole country of Iran and had topographical codes in color to denote the elevation of areas above sea level.

"You will have to involve several others in your mission, but only you two will have complete knowledge of the plan. I know you will want to have Jefe and Alita involved and that is fine, of course. They can play a vital role in this, although they will not know much detail. Jefe's contacts will be critical. We have a short time envelope here and he can get us the people where we need them to be in short order."

"I thought this would be an ideal place for us to get our heads together to work on a problem that has come up. I had this place swept for bugs and mikes just this morning. This chalet was once owned by Gerald Ford and we bought it from the guy who bought it from him. It has pretty good security provisions, but we have brought it up to date," said the President.

His study overlooked the valley and had a terrific view.

"Sometimes it is difficult to concentrate here with this view, but we manage," he said.

"I can see why one might be distracted," said Lero. "The view is magnificent."

The President looked down at the chart of Iran on the conference table. There were several sites marked with stick on labels.

"These are all the nuclear program related sites that we know about. We are confident that there are others because the elves are constantly at work improving and de-centralizing their facilities."

He motioned for them to sit and they took chairs around the table.

"The reason I asked you both to meet me here is that last week we received information from one of our assets that a team of scientists has completed work on the triggering device for a nuclear weapon and we think that they will test it soon. If the test is successful, then the Nuclear Club will have a new member."

He let that information soak in for a moment.

"What we don't know is where they have built the trigger, where they intend to mate it up with the device to create the nuclear weapon, where they intend to test it, and how they intend to transport the trigger to the device and the device to the test site. "

"We are pretty confident that they will test the device underground to keep it a secret. Our people at the

Overhead Reconnaissance Office have given us a list of sites where the test might be conducted, but right now, the whole thing is a puzzle with several variables."

"What I want you two to do is come up with a way to disable the trigger or destroy it on its way to be mated to the device, or set the device off before the elves intend it so as to eliminate their key scientists and their accumulated fissionable material."

There was a long silence around the table.

Lero was the first to speak. "Now that we know the problem, we need to assess the assets we have to counter the threat. Have you given thought to how you want the interdiction to take place, sir?" he asked the President.

"Well, as you know, we want this effort to be cagey as possible. We want to approach in stealth, strike quickly, and leave them wondering where the strike came from and who is responsible, or whether their own ineptitude caused the device to detonate before they intended."

"If we strike using aircraft, even like the Israelis did using that captured Egyptian Mirage III, they will detect an incoming flight, in all probability, because, also in all probability, the test they are planning will take place substantially inland, so an aircraft approaching would most likely be detected even if it is not prevented from striking. On the other hand, if we use a missile, they can analyze the metal from the debris field and determine the source. If the time line is short, we probably won't have time to insert teams at the anticipated places and sneaking the weaponry inland that far would be a serious challenge."

"I agree," said the President. "Although you and the Israelis proved last time that using laser designators and smart bombs worked quite well, in a strike near the shore of the Persian Gulf, but I agree with you that an aircraft strike in like this is not a good idea this time."

"What other details can you tell us now, sir?" asked Lero.

"Well, before you extricated her, Nadja sent us information about the probable location of the test site. Her boss, Dr. Hassani at Azad University, is thought by us to be the chief of the trigger design and construction project. This information indicates that the government started preparing an abandoned salt mine about a hundred miles south east of Isfahan for a test site. What we don't know is if they intend to transport the trigger to the assembly site of the device or directly to the test site for assembly onto the device. We believe with a high level of confidence that the trigger is being prepared in the Physics Department of Azad University at a facility in Tehran. Keep in mind that Azad University is the third largest such institution in the world and is the world's largest private university system. It was brought together by our old nemesis, Ali Akbar Hashemi Rafsanjani in 1982."

At this point, Janice who has sat silently through the briefing so far, spoke up.

"Our analysts believe that if the assembly takes place at the site where the weapon is being built, it will take place at Fordo, near Qom. Then they would have to transport the completed device to the test site. If we are correct that they will use the site in the salt mine southeast of Isfahan, they will have to transport the device over three hundred miles. However, if we strike the device after it is completely assembled, but before it reaches the test site, we may inadvertently trigger the device and cause a nuclear event out in the open in central Iran."

Jean asked, "What are the chances that an explosion such as a strike by a bomb or a missile will set off the device?"

"Well," continued Janice. "a direct hit would have a probability of about eighty percent of detonating the device. A hit close, such as within fifty yards with a conventional bomb or missile would only have a ten percent probability of detonating the device, but could scatter radioactive material over a square mile, with lots of atmospheric spreading in the resulting blast cloud."

"Clearly," said the President, "It would be preferable to strike the trigger before it gets to the device wherever that event is planned to take place."

"So we are looking at a probable route from Tehran to Fordo, then?" asked Lero.

"Yes," said the President, "But we don't know when they will transport it or what route they will use, direct or indirect."

"What is the suspected time line of the test?" asked Lero.

"We think they will be in a position to start putting the components together within the next six weeks," said the President.

There was a pause before anyone spoke.

"I have an idea for you to evaluate. I want you to visit with Professor Ernest Galvin at the University of Arizona in Tempe. He is privy to a system that you may choose to use. Please report to me as soon as you can meet with him and evaluate what he tells you. I am looking to the two of you to devise our response to this situation. As you can appreciate, this needs to be kept most secret. Get in touch as soon as you have met with him and when you have some suggestions about procedure."

The President took out his cell phone and dialed a number stored in it.

"This is Mr. Murfree. May I speak to Professor Galvin?"

After a pause, he said, "Ernie, this is Mr. Murfree. Say the word, please."

He paused while that was done. Then, he said. "What is your twenty?" (Location)

"Very well, can you meet with two of my associates about that matter we discussed earlier?"

Another pause, then he said: "Alright. These two people are highly trained technically and I am sure you will have no difficulty communicating with them. I will ask them to be at your office at ten Tuesday morning. They will use the code word: 'Ottawa.' Thanks, Ernie. Give my regards to Irene. Bye."

Lero and Jean exchanged a look.

"My friend cannot meet with you until Tuesday morning. His office is in Tempe, Arizona, at the University. You will find him at this address." The President handed Lero a card with an address and telephone number on it.

"Janice and I have to return to Washington today. Why don't you all stay in Vail and enjoy the place over the weekend and fly down to Tempe on Monday to see Ernie on Tuesday morning? Here is a pouch of 'homework' for you to study before you meet with Ernie. We have copies of everything that is in here. There is a thermite device that will incinerate the pouch and its contents if anyone but you tries to open it. There is a digital pad on the side. Input the four digit code before you open the flap. If you don't do that, it will self destruct in twenty seconds."

"We know where you are staying and a man will be watching your place whenever you leave it over the weekend. They will not bother you and will keep their distance when you are in your quarters, but will make sure that this pouch remains our secret until you leave to go to Tempe. When you leave, one of our guys will meet you at the airport, ostensibly to reclaim the car which you will be using during your visit here. Give him the pouch and it will be transmitted to you at your headquarters by a military courier this week. In order to be sure that you are giving the pouch to an authorized person, ask for the word. The word is 'Fairbanks.' Any other word will reveal someone who has not authority and may be a foreign agent. Our people will be watching their man obtain the pouch from you, so there will probably be no problem. Sorry about all the cloak and dagger stuff, but this is critically important."

"Now, let us let you two go and enjoy your weekend in Vail," said the President as he and the First Lady rose to see them out.

"I will set up a meeting soon to review our plans, so you may need to come east for that."

"That would be no problem, sir," said Lero.

The President shook Lero's hand and looked at him and Jean earnestly.

"I am so glad we have you to rely on. God be with you."

Lero and Jean nodded, and said their goodbyes to the Thompsons. They walked down the stairs and out into the parking circle with the pouch held by Jean between them.

Chapter 9

Once they had registered and gotten to their rooms, they decided to look for a place to have lunch and tour a bit before they ended up there. Lero put the pouch in the drawer beside the bed and they went out in jeans and jackets to explore Vail. Lero thought he saw the "watchers" in a dark brown Ford LTD across from the hotel parking lot. The windows were tinted, so he could not see in. He smiled and opened the door for Jean. They had enough time to take the cable car to the upper lodge before lunch and were pleased to find that they could have lunch there. The view was magnificent. It was a clear day and they could see fifty miles easily. There was just a light breeze and it did not even rustle the wax paper under their fish and chips. Jean had a glass of Chardonnay and Lero had an O'Douls. They relaxed and enjoyed the view, trying not to think about what awaited them and each wanting the other to enjoy the day and relax.

When they got back to the rooms after a great afternoon of shopping in Vail and sight seeing, they decided it was a good time to open the pouch and begin to study up.

Jean input the four digit code and counted to ten before opening the leather flap. Inside the pouch were several envelopes of differing thicknesses. Lero gave the top one to Jean and took the second. They opened each like kids would open a birthday present, eager to learn what each contained.

Jean's envelope had a dossier on Ernie Galvin. Born in Lynchburg, Virginia, 1955. Bachelors at the Naval Academy, 1977. Tour of duty on a destroyer in the Mediterranean. Masters in Physics at Duke, 1982. Ph.D. in Nuclear Physics from Princeton, 1986. Resumed Naval Career, promoted through the ranks to Admiral in 1996. Had a disabling stroke in 2006 and retired from active duty. Hired as Physics Professor, University of Arizona, 2007. Married to Joanne for forty one years, grown children and teenaged grandchildren. Research director for the University in the Physics Department. Top security clearance. The picture showed an alert, focused man with a high forehead, thinning blonde hair and piercing blue eyes.

"Not all great patriots are in uniform," she thought.

Jean's envelope had a history of the production of nuclear triggers, stating with the one that Robert Oppenhiemer and his cohorts put together in 1945, through the latest technology. By the time she read through the pages, she had a good grasp of the technology. It is so much easier to grasp the technology when it is laid out in historical form, than it is to conceive and achieve the next step in technology. Surely there would be further developments in nuclear triggers, but now she knew what comprised the present state of the art and was ready to move onto the next envelope.

They switched envelopes and studied what the other had just read. As they read, the sun set over the mountains, bathing their room in golden light. The change in light lifted their attention from their studies and they went to the window to look out at Vail and the sunset. It was a red, gold moment.

After they had studied into the early evening. She asked him if he wanted to go out for a bite to eat.

I'm not really hungry. Are you?" he asked.

"No, that was such a nice lunch. I am still not hungry. You look like you need a nice soak in the hot tub. Why don't I fill it and put a nice candle in the bathroom. You can study some more and join me when I get everything ready.

"That is a great idea, except I would rather watch you do those things than sit here and study. I especially want to watch you pick what to change into before the hot tub."

"That is so sweet and considerate of you. I would rather wear that small silver necklace with the turquoise gem you bought me this afternoon into the tub. I like to take off my clothes long enough before we get in the tub so that the marks made by garments have time to disappear. I want to look my best for you."

"Jean, I am such a lucky man. You are so much woman. I am entranced by you. I love to watch you move. I dream about you when we are apart. You have cast quite a spell on me."

"I am so glad," she smiled and got up to go to the bedroom to begin preparations. She bent over and gave him a big juicy kiss on the neck before she ambled over to the bedroom door.

By the time the hot tub was full, the room had an aura of hot steamy water. A gentle steamy look filled the room. The candle Jean had chosen was in a holder that obscured it from direct sight, but it reflected on the tiled wall of the bathroom, giving a warm, amber ambiance. When he came in, Jean was standing in the tub, wearing his favorite outfit. My, she was beautiful. A wave went through him as he approached. As he stepped down into the tub, she reached over to him and pulled herself against him and kissed him very thoroughly.

Chapter 10

It was a very special, unforgettable evening.

When he awakened in the morning, the first thing he saw was Jean kneeling on the bed next to him, smiling sweetly, still in his favorite outfit. He reached for her waist and pulled her to him.

She asked, "Would you help me with the moisturizing lotion?"

"Sure," he said, "Do you want the quick overall application or the slow and thorough application that your dermatologist recommended?

"Take at least a couple of hours. It should have time to soak in before I let you sponge it off of me in the shower. I like your thoroughness," she said with a wicked smile.

When it came time to leave, they checked out and drove the borrowed car to the airport. They pulled into the parking lot next to another dark colored LTD. There were two men sitting in the parked car. Jean and Lero got out and got their bags from the trunk. As they passed by the parked car, one of the men rolled down his window and asked, "Pardon me, did you see a brown pouch nearby?"

Lero responded, "Yes, it is on the front seat. The keys are in the ignition. Thanks."

"Thank you, sir. Have a nice flight."

When they got into the reception area of the fixed base operator, he glanced back toward the parking lot and noticed the Ford being backed out of its parking slot.

Lero asked the lady at the counter to have the lineman top up the tanks with 100LL, aviation gasoline. She talked to her lineman on a walkie talkie and in due time, the tank truck pulled over in front of the Comanche and the lineman took out the hose to fuel their plane.

Jean and Lero wheeled their roll around bags out to the Comanche as the lineman was putting his hose away.

"All four tanks topped, sir," said the lineman. "Took sixty two gallons."

"Good, thanks," said Lero and they opened the luggage compartment door and began putting their bags away. As Jean completed putting their gear away and getting the flight equipment ready, Lero walked back into the FBO and paid the lady for the fuel and the overnight fees.

After the normal preliminaries, they taxied out to the active runway. The radios got set on the proper navigation aids and communications frequencies and he got the altimeter setting on the Unicom frequency. The nice lady also said that there was no reported inbound traffic.

The run-up to check the magnetos went fine and he asked Jean if she were ready to go. She asked: "Did you check everything?" He nodded and they exchanged a kiss.

Even though it had a one degree downslope, they had chosen to take off to the west, into the prevailing wind. Lero announced on the radio, "Eagle County Unicom, Eagle County Traffic, Comanche seven niner papa is taking the active at Eagle County, departing west bound toward Snow VOR, red over white."

As they reached the center line of the runway, Lero advanced the throttle to the stop and the Comanche began to eat up the runway. Because of the altitude of the runway, it took about forty percent longer in time and distance to take off compared to their normal takeoff at Davis Monthan, but the little twin lifted off smoothly and took to the morning air.

"We'll just fly the flight route we came up on, but at Zuni, we will go more westward and land at Sky Harbor in Phoenix," he said.

"Okay," she said into the intercom.

"Denver center, Comanche seven seven seven niner papa, off Eagle County, climbing to ten thousand five hundred, squawking twelve hundred," Lero said into the mike.

"Comanche seven seven seven niner papa, Denver Center, squawk three three two two and ident, please. Say intentions."

Lero keyed his mike. "Seven niner papa is VFR to Phoenix Sky Harbor. Appreciate flight following if you have the time today."

"Roger, seven niner papa, radar contact, say number of souls on board and hours of fuel, please."

"Seven niner papa has two souls on board, six hours of fuel."

"Roger, seven niner papa, we show your mode C readout at eight thousand seven hundred."

(Note: Mode C is the separate signal of the transponder that tells the ground radar the present altitude above sea level of the aircraft. It is an interface between an altitude sensing transducer and a radio. It sends a signal to the ground radio whenever the transponder is interrogated by the ground radar.)

"Seven niner papa, roger, thanks."

"There is Snow VOR," said Jean.

"Sure enough," said Lero. "Why don't you take the yoke and fly us to Sky Harbor?" he asked.

"Really? I'd love to," said Jean as she put her right hand on the yoke.

Lero put the clip board with the VOR and Center and Approach control frequencies on it between them so she could see it clearly.

"Level off at ten five," he instructed as he went into a mode to watch her fly the plane.

At ten thousand, she began slowly pulling the throttles back to twenty two inches of manifold pressure and to trim nose down to stop their climb and level off. By the time they got to ten five, she had pulled the propeller controls back to set the revolutions at twenty four hundred.

As they passed over Snow VOR, she turned them left a bit to straighten the course line to Junction City VOR.

"Comanche seven niner papa, you have Cessna traffic opposite direction at eleven thousand five hundred, twelve o'clock and four miles."

"Roger, Center, seven niner papa is looking, thanks," said Jean into the mike.

As they looked for it, Lero said, "I have him. Slightly to the right and clearly above us."

"I see him, too," said Jean and keyed her mike.

"Center, seven niner papa has the traffic."

"Seven niner papa, roger," said Denver Center.

As they few out between the mountains, Lero said, "I see the Junction City VOR. Straight ahead, about seven miles."

"Good," said Jean, as she twisted the dial of the second navigation radio from the frequency for the Snow VOR to the frequency for the Cortez VOR ahead of them to the south.

In three hours, they had Sky Harbor Airport in sight. They had been on flight following all the way and had been handed over to Phoenix Approach in due course. After they landed, they taxied to the fixed base operator. They told the lineman that they would be overnight and would order fuel before they left. They got a cab and went to the Tempe Campus.

Chapter 11

The secretary of the Physics department called Ernie for them and he told her to let them come down to his office. The secretary gave them a key to use in the elevator so they could access the second sub-basement. Ernie met them at the elevator door.

"Good to meet you both," he said as he shook hands with them. "Come on back to my office. I am anxious to hear about your project."

The cool and dimly lit corridor led them to a non-descript door with the numbers one zero eight on it. Ernie unlocked with a pass key, and stood aside for them to enter.

He motioned them to chairs at a conference table and joined them across from their chairs.

Once they were sure that they were alone with Ernie, Jean asked; "Mr. Murfree told us to ask you to bring us up to speed on Module 18. Has he told you about our interest?"

"Yes, he and I talked last night. I will start wherever you want and tell you anything I know."

"We were given this brown pouch full of information about the Module and we have been studying diligently, but we really need someone familiar to start at the beginning and bring us up to date, including its capabilities."

"This is really complicated," she said, as she looked. "Partly because it is so long ago and partly because it is so primitive. It appears it will be like trying to talk to a cave dweller."

"Tell me what you mean," said Ernie.

"Well, we know that Module Eighteen contains missiles. We know that none have been used before. We know that some are nukes and some are high explosives. We know that they have been there since the late eighties or maybe nineteen ninety. . We know that the only way to communicate with Module Eighteen is by radio signals on the correct frequencies. If it were a video game, it would be much easier."

Ernie said, "I think when Gorbachev told Reagan about Module Eighteen, he was dealing in good faith, revealing what the Russkies had, but not giving Reagan anything that he could use to hack the Module's controls."

Lero asked, "So even if you found out the correct frequency or frequencies, you would need to know what to say to the onboard computer to get it to do what you want?"

"That's right," said Ernie. "But we have a very important piece of information. When our astronauts shared a tour on Mir, the Russian Space Station, the Russians made the mistake of including a Manual on the operation of Module Eighteen in with the other operations manuals on board. We think this was a mistake and not done intentionally. Remember, no one but Gorby and a very few Russians knew about Module Eighteen and that was in the eighties, twenty years before the tour on Mir. Even if they read the manual, they would have no way of knowing which satellite Module Eighteen was a part of or what Module Eighteen was capable of, let alone being able to communicate with it and command it to do anything."

"But the frequencies were still a dark mystery. We studied the frequencies used by the Russians on all of their satellites, and there were thousands, as you know, over the twenty years. However, we learned that the Russians always used one band of frequencies in the eighteen hundred megahertz range. This, alone, kept most of my graduate students busy for years while they took courses to complete their graduate degrees. Each of the ones I chose would put in lots of hours at the lab gathering information and tracking these Russian satellites. Almost all of my graduate students here were active military, assigned here to get a graduate degree in a useful discipline, and they all had top secret clearances. Even then, I kept from them any information that would reveal the existence of Module Eighteen. Since Module Eighteen never has broadcast, there were no loose frequencies to analyze or explain. Just keeping track of the grant money required an additional two staff members. It was all run out of the second sub-basement of this building, but we had a nice antenna array on the roof. We could access any of the el-int gathering equipment and data from Fort Huachuca down in the southern mountains, too."

(Note to the detail inclined: Fort Huachuca is home to the United States Army Intelligence Command and is co-located with Sierra Vista Civilian airport. It has a working population of eighteen thousand workers daily. The runway was an alternate for the space shuttle and is over twelve thousand feet long. The U. S. Army Network Enterprise Technical Command (Netcom) is headquartered there. It is only about twenty two miles from the Arizona-Mexican Border and is the primary el-int collection facility for radio broadcasts and telemetry over the southern hemisphere and elsewhere. They maintain an unmarked aerostat ((cable tethered balloon)) with antennas at fifteen thousand feet for such purposes.)

Lero and Jean exchanged a glance. They were obviously impressed with the breadth and depth of the program. They were quickly becoming aware of just how crucial an asset Ernie was.

"The pouch you have is the same one that Mikhail Gorbachev gave President Reagan on or about December first, nineteen eighty six. Just as the Soviet Union was collapsing, he gave the information about Module Eighteen to President Reagan so it would not fall into the hands of the hot headed Russian KGB leaders and top military leaders and maybe start a war. We don't know if President Reagan gave him anything in return, but our belief is that he did not. We believe that it was sort of a 'safe keeping' thing as well as a gesture of friendship after they had gotten off to a rocky start at Reykijvik."

"You can imagine the technological challenge this was for us. All of our research had to be doubly secretive because we dared not let the Russians find out that we knew about Module Eighteen and we did not want any of them to learn it existed. If they had found out, it might have been used at a critical time and might have changed recent history significantly. We had to translate the manual into English, and as you know from your capacities and training in languages, there are many times when a skillful interpreter is needed to accurately convey into English what is written or said in Russian or any other language. The nuances can be critical. As we learned about Module Eighteen, we built a program to accumulate our knowledge. Of course, we concealed the true nature and location of the Module, and we used our own code names for various components. Remember Russian has a Cyrillic alphabet and sometimes there is no English equivalent to a character in Russian, but with the discovery of this manual we were able to crack the code, so to speak. Now we knew which frequency to use to talk to Module Eighteen. The next thing was to learn what to say.

The first signal is a wake-up call, essentially saying to Module Eighteen, "Hey, wake up. Acknowledge." If it gets such a message, it does a systems check, like a computer boot, and then it broadcasts a set response in Morse Code to indicate that it is awake and ready to receive commands. Remember also, that, contrary to the Outer Space Treaty of 1967 to refrain from placing weapons of mass destruction on satellites or using atomic powered systems in their satellites, this Module has a Cesium 137 powered battery that has a design useful life of sixty five years."

"So what is the procedure to launch one of the missiles from the Module?" asked Jean.

Ernie continued, "After the wake-up call and the acknowledgement, you instruct the Module to electronically "choose" on or more of the missiles. It then acknowledges that it is connected to that or those missiles. You then give it an instruction to begin powering up the guidance gyros in the missile or missiles. It then acknowledges that signal. Then it pauses until the gyros and onboard computers have fully booted and are ready for instructions. Once you receive that message, you input the coordinates on earth that you wish the missile or missiles to strike. This is done digitally and in Morse Code in a particular way: north or south latitude first, in degrees, minutes and seconds and hundredths of seconds. This is eight digits after the South or North Code. Then the computer loads this data and reports ready to receive again. Next, you input the Longitude. This is three digits for degrees, then two for minutes, then two for seconds and two more for hundredths after the East or West code. Because the satellite is geo-stationary, you don't have to worry about losing radio contact because it has traveled beyond the radio horizon."

"Have you every powered up Module Eighteen?" asked Jean. Lero leaned forward slightly in anticipation of Ernie's answer.

"No, in all the years I have known about Module Eighteen, I have never been asked to do that. Remember this is a secret operation that very few people have known about. President Reagan set up a procedure so that during the Presidency of any Democrats, the secret would be kept by me and one other person to be passed onto the next Republican President. I first found out about Module Eighteen in the spring of 1986 just after I completed my Ph.D. I was a Commander in the Navy at the time, assigned to Dahlgren Test Center in Virginia. I know they vetted me carefully, but they gave me no clue in advance about what my assignment would be. One afternoon, after lunch mess, I was summoned to the base commander's office. When I reported, I was ushered into his office, but he was not there. I quickly realized that I was in the presence of Ronald Reagan, the President and Admiral Starkey, the director of the Overhead Intelligence Bureau, although it was not called that just yet. They gave me the pouch with all the papers and manuals about Module Eighteen and told me that I would be the custodian of those papers until further notice and that the three of us would be the only people other than the few Soviets who knew about Module Eighteen. I was to study and prepare myself to communicate with Module Eighteen and, in time, train my replacement, once he or she was chosen. Otherwise, once we figured out how to communicate with Module Eighteen, I was to write the protocol for communications and simply stand by if I were ever needed."

"It must have been pretty tedious," said Jean.

"Yes, it was. But early on we devised a program to broadcast in Morse from a conventional key board. Just hit the key for a letter and the computer would generate the Morse code for that letter. We soon found that we needed to type slowly so the Morse generator could keep up, but we got the hang of it. Later, we devised a recording device that would take typewritten input as fast as one could type, but would relay it to the satellite at the desired slower speed. I need to teach you how to use that," he said.

"The responsibility must have kept you awake some nights," said Jean, and Lero nodded.

"Yes, it did, but it was such an honor to be chosen and it was such a fascinating task that, in time, I grew used to it and was able to resume my usual duties smoothly," he said.

"So basically, the Russians don't know they have Module Eighteen?" asked Jean.

"That's right," said Ernie. "Undoubtedly Gorbachev remembers about it, but he would not tell them now because it would reveal his complicity. They would probably find a way to eliminate him if they knew. The scientist who created Module Eighteen died of natural causes in nineteen ninety five and the general who knew about it disappeared in the aftermath of the collapse of the Soviet Union," said Ernie.

"How many people know about Module Eighteen now?" asked Lero.

"Counting you two, seven," said Ernie.

There was a pause.

Chapter 12

"What is the next step in the procedure after you input the latitude and longitude of the target?" asked Jean.

"Well, once the missile is chosen or missiles are chosen and spun up and programed with the latitude and longitudes, the computer will report to you with a string signal that it is ready to launch. Then you give it a code to tell it that you are ready to launch. At this point, it will ask for a "go code." This is an eight digit code string that tells the computer that you have authority to launch the missiles. Once it recognizes the "go code," it will expect you to either tell it to launch or to stand down, which will result in the computer cutting the power to the missiles so that their hard drives and gyros will spin down and the latitude and longitude information will be lost. If no launch code is received within ninety minutes, a coded inquiry will come from the computer in Module Eighteen asking if you still want it to stand by ready to launch. You must confirm you want it to continue on stand by within five minutes, or it will shut down, and go to sleep again."

"How many missiles are on Module Eighteen," asked Lero.

"There are eight. Three twenty kiloton devices, two ten kiloton devices and three high explosive devices," said Ernie.

"What generation of devices are they?" asked Lero.

"These are fifth generation devices, which were the standard first line Soviet weapons for the period from about 1980 to 1991."

"What satellite is Module Eighteen on and when was it launched?" asked Lero.

"Module Eighteen was attached to the Yantar 4K2 satellite, otherwise known as Kobalt. It was designed at Zhelenogorsk and assembled at Omsk and launched as a Kosmos satellite to keep it secret, number 1201, from the Plesesk Cosmodrome Complex 200, Pad 39 on January 20, 1981. The original launch weight of seven thousand kilograms was increased by six metric tonnes, so they had to burn the booster longer to get it into orbit. Because of the heavy weights of the missile launchers and the satellites they launched, the Russians had to build a railroad north to Milny. That, in itself was a major engineering feat. Building anything on the permafrost is touchy. Module 18 is in one of the highest orbits they used for the Cosmos Series."

Jean asked, "Is the Plesetsk cosmodrome associated with Baikonur?"

"No," said Ernie. "Plesetsk is about two hundred miles north of Moscow. It is in high, but relatively flat terrain, in a typical dark Russian pine forest. It was developed as a site for Russian intercontinental missiles in the fifties. It is located with a small town built by the Russians, call Milny, which means 'peace.' Plesetsk was not given the prominence of Baikonur in the early years because it was not capable of launching the larger Soviet rockets. Once the Soviet Union split up, the Kazaks demanded such a high rent for Baikonur that the Russians began upgrading Plesetsk and using it more. It is not as good for launching geostationary orbiting satellites as Baikonur, but it is well located for trans-polar launches because any debris from launch boosters will fall into the White Sea and not impact populated areas. Since the breakup of the Soviet Union, the Russians have poured lots of money into Plesetsk. Nowadays, there are, at any given time, about three thousand people living at Plesetsk. The fact that you were not familiar with Plesetsk is testament to the success of the Russians' penchant for secrecy. They are the most paranoid people on earth about secrecy."

"Just curious, did George H. W. Bush know about Module Eighteen before he became President?" asked Lero.

"No," said Ernie, without expression. "However, once he became the President elect, I was tasked to brief him after the election of 1988. At that point, there were four of us who knew about Module Eighteen."

"How long would it take for one of the missiles from Module Eighteen to reach a point on earth?" asked Lero.

"The three different warheads all accelerate at different rates. The rockets propelling the missiles are all the same. So the time is slightly different for each class. At normal speeds, they would reach the surface of a point directly below the satellite in fifty six minutes, give or take a minute or two because of weight differentials Remember we are talking about an orbit of approximately twenty two thousand miles above the earth and you are talking about a target within an arc of eight thousand miles. If the target were near the edge of that part of the earth that is visible from the satellite, it would take up to eighteen minutes longer, because the straight line distance from the satellite would be increased by the deflection from the straight down angle and the curvature of the earth," Ernie answered.

"Where, in general, is your probable target?" asked Ernie.

"Central Disneyland," said Jean. "Mr. Murfree has intel that indicates that the elves have a trigger for a nuclear device and they want to test it very soon. He has asked us to interfere with the test."

"You are not thinking of using a nuclear device are you," asked Ernie, a bit anxiously.

"No, indeed," said Lero. "We just want to interdict the trigger somewhere between where it is being built and the test site, or, failing that, at the test site."

"Well, if the trigger is on or in a vehicle that is moving, there will be a slight problem. Once the strike coordinates are loaded in the missile, there is no way to reprogram the missile in flight. That would be like shooting a bird on the wing, don't you think?" asked Ernie.

"Well, if we cannot reprogram the missile in flight, can we tell the missile to hit a target that is being painted by a laser designator?" asked Lero.

Ernie studied a moment, scratched his chin, looked at the ceiling as if trying to read the answer there, then said, "Yes, we could do that, but the target would have to be within a rather narrow arc of deflection from the originally entered coordinates. The missiles cannot detect a painted target using any of the laser designators we have until it is within about fifty miles."

Lero asked: "Can we disarm the missile after launch? Can you destroy it in flight?"

'The nuclear tipped missile can be disarmed in flight, and destroyed. The high explosive tipped missiles can be exploded in flight," said Ernie.

Lero asked, "How far from the programmed target do you think we could rely on if we use the laser designator?"

Ernie studied a moment and answered, "About two miles, provided that you have the laser designator painting the target when the missile comes within fifty miles."

There was another pause while Lero and Jean digested their astonishment at what Ernie said.

"How long would it take the missile to reach the target if it were redirected by the laser designator at a fifty mile distance, assuming it could deflect enough to hit the target?" asked Jean.

Again, Ernie studied a moment and said, matter-of-factly, "About ten seconds."

There was a substantial pause.

Jean spoke first.

"I can see that we need to do a lot of catching up. May I camp out here to get you to bring me up to speed?" she asked.

"Sure," said Ernie. "We have rooms for our graduate students here in the building. Some are vacant now. You can stay right here."

"Good," said Jean.

"It is really fortunate that you are so close to our base at Davis Monthan, sir," said Lero. "Now, it appears that we need to get to work finding a crew of people with laser designators and getting them into Disneyland between where we think the trigger is being built and where we think they will try a test," said Lero. "Jean, you stick close here as you proposed, and work with Ernie while I go back to base and try to get a team ready to infiltrate Disneyland. If there are three places involved, the trigger shop, the nuclear device shop and the test site, we may have a lot of territory to cover, not to mention the task of getting a team with designators in there and out of there after the party."

Jean reluctantly but immediately agreed. She said, "Why don't you take the Comanche back to base, so you can get work immediately and I will stick here and try to learn as much as I can before the magic moment."

Ernie nodded his agreement.

"Ordinarily, I don't like to move so fast, but that is an excellent idea and we need to move fast here. Ernie, it was a pleasure and an education to meet you and visit with you. Thank you for your service to our country. I will walk out to the car with Jean and bring her bags back in here and go on to base. Hopefully, I will see you both soon," said Lero.

Ernie walked out with Lero to the elevator while Jean finished putting a few things into her brief case. Once they were alone, Ernie said, "This is touchy business. We don't know how much high explosive is aboard those missiles. Our best guess is five hundred kilograms. Based on our knowledge of Soviet explosive development at the time those were manufactured, if it is five hundred kilograms there could be a fireball about a thousand feet across and the heat wave and pressure wave would be substantial. Protect yourself well. You will be danger close in order to get into range for the laser designator. As soon as you see the flash, get behind something substantial."

"Thanks," said Lero. "Don't tell Jean, OK?"

"Well, alright," said Ernie, "But just be careful. If the missile is off much at all, it could be hazardous to your health." They shook hands solemnly.

Just then Jean walked up from the laboratory. Lero held the elevator door open while she approached.

(Technical note: 'Danger close' is a term used by our infantry and others to denote that a soldier is close enough to the intended target that there is 'enhanced danger' of injury or worse. When a troop on the ground calls in an airstrike in 'danger close' conditions, usually the pilot and troop exchange names in case an investigation is needed after the fact.)

Chapter 13

Lero thought to himself as he flew along toward Davis Monthan from Sky Harbor: "We cannot hit this thing on the road from the assembly site to the test site because we might set off a nuclear blast. We have to find out if the trigger is going to be sent to the site where it will be assembled into the weapon, or on its way to the test sight if they intend to put it on the weapon there. How in the world are we going to find that out in time?"

"Tucson Approach, November seven seven seven niner papa is thirty northwest, VFR, landing Davis Monthan, squawking twelve hundred at six thousand five hundred."

"Roger seven niner papa, Information Tango is current at Davis Monthan, maintain six thousand five hundred, fly heading one four five."

"Seven niner papa, roger, maintaining six thousand five hundred, on heading one four five."

In the clear air of southern Arizona, he could see the vast expanse of aircraft spread out over Davis Monthan Air Force Base ahead.

"Approach, seven niner papa has Davis Monthan in sight."

"Roger, seven niner papa,, contact Davis Monthan tower on one eighteen decimal niner, good day."

"Seven niner papa, roger, good day."

The tower vectored Lero and seven niner papa for a straight in approach to Runway One Two and he taxied to his hangar. Once the Comanche was chocked in its hangar and the door securely locked, he got in his Grand Cherokee to drive to his office. The route took him directly across the storage area where close to a thousand aircraft were parked in neat rows, plastic sheeting covering windscreens and tires and plugs in the engine intakes.

Once he got back into his Quonset hut office building and sat down at his desk, the enormity of the task ahead of him really hit him.

"How in the world are we going to find out when they intend to move the trigger assembly and where they will take it?" he thought. "How am I going to get a team of operatives into Iran that quickly and how can we get weapons and laser designators in there with them?"

Instinctively, he reached for his satellite phone. The earpiece emitted its usual non-descript hum after he dialed. Then the distinct click and the ring tone began. After five rings, a sleepy Jefe answered.

"Hello."

"Hello, say the word, please."

"Sedona. What is the good word?"

"Houston."

"What's up?"

"Party in Disneyland. I need you to help me with the guest list."

"What kind of costumes will be required?

"I need six people comfortable in Disneyland. The party may go on for a couple of weeks. No fireworks, but potential rapid travel."

"When does the party start?"

"I would love to get everybody together for a pre-party warm up as early as this Monday."

"Let me make some calls. Does the party have a theme?"

"Yes, We are calling it 'Hoopla.'"

"Sounds appropriate.

"What is your twenty?"

"The summer place."

Another thing, are you confident that our conversations are scrambled? I want to ask you something sensitive and I don't know how to put it into any form but correct English."

"Yes, this phone is good to go. I had it checked on the way over here."

"Okay," said Lero. "I need to know whom I need to talk to for a map of locations of arms caches and contents in Disneyland."

"Major David Browning at JSOC Headquarters at Fort Bragg would know that."

"Great. Thanks. Get some rest."

"Call day or night."

"Okay, best to you both."

"You, too. Bye."

Jefe dialed a number and waited while it rang twice.

"Hello," was the only greeting.

"Tell Mr. Knight that Jefe needs six familiar and comfortable in Disneyland for a two week party, leaving your place Friday evening."

"Will do. Shall we confirm the availability?"

"Yes, I will be waiting for your call."

"Very well. Good day."

Jefe held the phone for a moment before he put it back in the shade of the umbrella over the table. He looked over at the pool and the ocean below. He was thankful for his little hideaway on Keros and he was very thankful for Alita lying on her favorite air mattress next to the pool, asleep in the sun with only a scarf over her eyes to protect her from the Greek sun. He decided to just sit and watch her breathe rather than go back to the air mattress and chance waking her.

Chapter 14

Jean had been studying the contents of the pouch in Ernie's office. He returned from teaching a graduate class in astrophysics and sat down gratefully. He used a cane when he ambled about the office and when he went to teach or to leave and go home. He was lean, and strong, but there was a bit of his control capability missing and he had kind of a halting walk and his balance was imperfect.

Ernie said to Jean, "You know, while I was teaching just now, a thought came to me about the present dilemma. We may choose to use one of the smaller nukes to make this strike to make it seem like their device went off accidently. Why don't you run the idea by Lero and see how he feels about it and you definitely should confer with Mr. Murfree about the idea, too."

Jean had that deer in the headlights look for a few seconds, before her training and her processor kicked in. She tried to conceal her astonishment and almost succeeded.

Ernie paused a bit and then said: "My belief is that they will pick a cave or a tunnel in a remote area in the southeastern desert for the test. The trip the device and the trigger will have to make will probably be a long one, whether they are mated together before or at the test site. There is no way to know these things, but we much keep our minds open to all possibilities and sort out the probabilities, don't you think?"

"Of course," said Jean. "I just hope that none of our people have to get too close to the test site. How many people do you think we should send in to have a good chance to succeed?"

"If I had my way, I would send in twenty, but we may not be able to do that."

"Do you want me to see if I can round up twenty laser designators and get them on their way to the theatre?" she asked.

"Good idea. Send them to Prince Sultan Air Base if you can. We will stage out of there."

Retired Vice Admiral William McRay, the former commandant of the Joint Special Operations Command, was sitting at a patio table next to his swimming pool lounging in the Virginia sun. His cell phone vibrated on the glass top of the table.

"Hello," he said.

"Admiral, this is Dan Roman. We met last fall when you visited some of our wounded service men in Qatar."

"Oh, yes, as I recall you had a leg injury. How is that healing?"

"Just fine, sir. I appreciated the visit and the other guys did, too, but that is not the reason for my call. Mr. Murfree has asked me to head up a party in Disneyland in the near future and I am going to need some personnel and some tactical advice. He recommended that I contact you."

"Fine," said Admiral McRay. "I take it that since you are contacting me, now that I have retired, Mr. Murfree wants to hold this party off the books."

"That is correct, sir. It will be by invitation only."

"What is you twenty?" asked McRay.

"Davis Monthan, in Tucson," said Lero.

"How soon do you want to meet?" asked McRay.

"At your earliest convenience, sir," said Lero.

"I happen to be coming into your neighborhood tomorrow. Why don't you meet me at Dallas Fort Worth Airport, the

Southwest Airlines Executive Club about two PM Dallas time?"

"That would be fine, sir. Thank you very much. See you then."

Dallas Fort Worth is huge, the largest airport, by acreage in the United States. Lero could see it from fifty miles away. He was talking to Fort Worth Center when he spotted it and said "Center, Seven niner papa has Dallas Fort Worth in sight."

"Roger, seven niner papa, contact Dallas Fort Worth Approach now on one two six decimal two five."

"Roger, Center, seven niner papa over to Approach. Thanks. Good day."

Then he twisted the dial of the communications radio and called: "Dallas Fort Worth Approach, Comanche seven seven seven niner papa with you level at six thousand five hundred, squawking 2435, landing Dallas Fort Worth."

"Comanche seven seven seven niner papa, Dallas Fort Worth Approach, squawk five zero five one and ident, please. Information Delta is current. Plan on left base to Runway three five left."

Lero repeated the instructions to Approach Control and tuned his second communications radio to the ATIS frequency.

"Seven niner papa, descend to and maintain three thousand, please."

"Seven niner papa down to three and maintain three," said Lero. By now, the huge expanse of DFW filled his windscreen. He could see a broad inverted cone of airplanes descending in the clear air toward DFW. He could see the numbers on the runway closest to him. Three Five, and below the numbers was a large L for left. DFW has three parallel runways and a cross runway, too. It is a very busy airport. They don't get much private air traffic and Lero was grateful for the good handling to get him on the ground where he could taxi to the Fixed Base Operator's place of business. He only needed about a sixth of the runway to bring seven niner papa down to taxiing speed.

"Seven niner papa, exit next taxiway, Contact ground when clear on point niner."

Lero acknowledged and when clear of the runway, he called Ground control.

"Dallas Fort Worth ground, Comanche seven niner papa clear of three five left, going to Stevens Aviation."

"Roger, seven niner papa, taxi to Stevens via taxiways Sierra and Tango, hold short of Runway three five Center."

Lero taxied up to the while line marking the edge of Runway three five center and called, "Ground, seven niner papa holding short at three five center."

"Roger, seven niner papa, hold short for landing MD-80 traffic on one mile final."

"Roger, seven niner papa, holding short."

Lero watched as the big twin jet made a nice landing about three hundred yards down the runway from his holding position. As the nose and cockpit of the MD-80 flashed by, he could see the pilot in the left seat, chin slightly raised like many pilots do to look over the panel on landing. An MD-80 lands on the mains with the nose gear about ten feet above the runway, then settles as the pilot lets it. He felt the blast of the wingtip vortices as they swept over his little plane and it rocked in response.

Once he got to Stevens Aviation, there was a lineman waiting for him to direct him to a spot in front of the building. When he crossed his arms, Lero stopped and cut the fuel to kill the engine. He opened the door to speak to the lineman.

"Will you be overnight, sir? And, will you require fuel?" asked the lineman.

"Probably overnight. I will call to order fuel before departure, thanks."

Lero post-flighted the Comanche, and tied the control yokes with a bungee cord to prevent damage from a gust of a passing plane and turned off the main switch. He unstrapped and climbed out onto the warm Dallas Fort Worth tarmac.

As he rolled his tote-bag into the reception room, the counter person greeted him with a beaming smile and asked if he needed ground transportation.

He smiled back at her and asked if there were a shuttle to the main terminal.

"Yes, sir. The shuttle will be by in about ten minutes. He will pull up at the rear door, blue Ford van.

"Thanks," said Lero and ambled over to the Men's Room to defuel.

Chapter 15

The guy in the van knew just where to drop Lero so he could walk pretty straight to the Southwest Airlines Executive Lounge. The nice lady in the booth next to the locked door looked up as he walked into range. She had a smile on her face as she asked, "Yes, can I help you?"

"I'm not a member, ma'am. I am here to meet a Mr. McRay."

She did not hesitate and buzzed him in. "Mr. McRay is seated in the lounge to your right. Have a nice visit," she said.

The ambiance inside was quite a bit quieter than the busy DFW terminal. There was thick carpet on the floor and there were sheer curtains in the windows. The lighting was indirect, from above and the colors were deep red and gold. The chairs scattered about were mostly nicely padded recliners where a fellow could nod off for an hour or so before catching his connecting flight.

As he approached, Admiral McRay rose from his seat to greet Lero.

"Good to meet you," he said and gestured Lero to a booth where they could sit closely and talk privately.

"If Mr. Murfree sent you, it must be important. What is the problem and how can I help?"

"First of all, thanks for seeing me so quickly. We are on a short leash here, sir," said Lero. "What I need is a team of twelve operators who are familiar with Disneyland. The operation involves infiltration, travel and use of electronic devices, but we hope to avoid any live fire. We want to destroy a particular item that will be in transit over what may turn out to be a wide area. That is why we need so many people. Our information source will hopefully be able to tell us with more particularity, but right now, it might be anywhere from Tehran to the desert southeast. We will be using laser designators paint the target. Heavy ordnance will be involved and it might be danger close."

"I don't have much more information to give you right now, but we were hoping you could find us a team of operators that are no longer in the military, but fresh enough to be familiar with weapons and tactics."

"There are several such people. Do you have a budget to cover twelve men for two months? They are not cheap, you know."

"If you could give me some idea of the money we would need, sir. I can give you assurances," said Lero.

"I would say that ten thousand per man per month would take care of it, plus expenses and you will provide all transportation and equipment."

"I think we can do that, sir. Do you want to handle the money or do you have someone to do that for you?"

"I would rather use an accounting firm in Fairfax. You can wire the money there. A deposit of about half in advance will be sufficient."

"Let me know the number of men and the amount at this number," said Lero and handed McRay an otherwise blank card with a telephone number and an email address written on it."

"Where will you want to initially meet with the men?" asked McRay.

"Somewhere central to the group. After you choose them and enlist them, let me know a city and we will make arrangements," said Lero. "I can tell you now that we will be staging out of Incirlik and that the men will need to report to the Athens Airport where transport to Incirlik will be provided."

"First of all, I cannot recommend staging out of Incirlik. There is too much potential for a security leak. Let me supply you later with an alternate staging site. I will also send you the contact information for a source for equipment for the men other than weapons. The proprietor is a long- time friend. Most, if not all of these operators have their own weapons and gear, but some will need weapons provided and they will need gear for the specific mission. I will provide you a dossier on each man by encrypted email. If you have any other needs, you can let me know by email."

"Thank you, sir. We appreciate your help. Jefe said to convey his personal regards, too."

"Jefe and I have worked together for years. He is a true patriot and a very effective operative. Tell him I said 'hello,' please."

"I will do that, Admiral. Again, thanks for your help."

"Glad to do it.," said McRay."If there are any problems, I will let you know. I will get back with you in the next few days. Good luck."

Both men rose to leave. They shook hands and Lero went out first. He thanked the nice lady at the entry door and never looked back.

Chapter 16

As he flew back to Tucson, his mind was buzzing with questions about the details of the project.

When he got home, Jean was waiting for him. The house smelled of roast chicken, and cornbread, his favorites. She told him that Ernie said she was current enough and could come back to bone up any time. He would stand by to help them when things got under way.

It was a nice time to catch up.

Once they had the meal, then went into the living room. She told him all about the set up that Ernie had at Tempe and he told here about his visit with Admiral McRay.

"How in the world are we ever going to intercept this trigger? It all depends on the informant. We have no idea how and by whom the trigger will be transported. There are almost infinite variables. How are we ever going to disperse our people to get a good chance at destroying the trigger?" she asked.

"I agree," he said. "If we don't get actionable intel from the informant, the whole thing will be for nothing."

Chapter 17

Sometimes, the fluorescent lights really got to Dr. Ferreydoon. He had spent the last two months here in the underground facility at Natanz. With no contact with the sun and the outside world, one could become stir crazy sometimes. He and the others took extra Vitamin D to supplement what the sun normally caused their bodies to produce. It was eight fifteen on a Wednesday, but the only way one could tell whether it was day or night was to consult one's watch or some other chromometer. His apartment in the dormitory section of the facility was at the far corner from the metallurgy group's department. The facility was so large that he could get a sufficient amount of exercise just walking from his dormitory room to the metallurgy department.

This morning, he had a little more skip in his step, though. Today was the day they were going to pour the enriched uranium into the mold that would comprise the fissile material for the first nuclear bomb that the facility, or the Islamic Republic, for that matter, would produce. Not even the Grand Ayatollah knew that today was the day, secrecy was so high.

He had last been in the furnace room the night before, to supervise the placement of the ingots into the furnace and the initiating of the melting cycle of the large electric cauldron they would use to melt the metal to pour the critical mass.

As he entered the lab, there was an air of joyful anticipation among the crew in attendance. This was the culmination of years of work and the whirling efforts of seven thousand Swedish centrifuges that worked constantly in the underground facility.

These centrifuges had separated the three percent of Uranium 235 from the majority of atoms of Uranium 238 in the uranium hexafluoride that each centrifuge contained. The separation took lots of time. It was almost like working in a whiskey distillery with all the waiting, but science had not come up with a better way to separate the U 235 from the U 238 than with centrifuges. Once the uranium ore was mined and crushed and concentrated, it was reacted with hydrofluoric acid in the presence of a catalyst to become uranium hexafluoride, a dark bluish liquid. Then the liquid was placed in the centrifuges to be whirled for long periods of time to extract the small percentage of U 235 hexafluoride from the U 238 hexafluoride. Then, when the U 235 concentration reached a certain level it was combined in another set of centrifuges down farther in the cascade. Ultimately, when a concentration of about ninety two percent U 235 was reached, the liquid was reacted with hydrogen, again in the presence of a catalyst and under high pressure, to reduce the compound back to metallic uranium. All of this had taken years. Only now, after all this time, did they have enough Uranium 235 to fabricate the core of the weapon, and today was the day that they would pour off the U 235 that had been melting in the cauldron overnight into the mold that they had meticulously prepared.

His shop foreman, Ali Akbar, greeted him with obvious enthusiasm.

"Allah be praised. This is a wonderful day, Dr. Ferreydoon," he said.

"Yes, Ali, thanks to you and all the people who have worked so hard here underground, today we will realize a long held ambition, thanks to Allah. Are the men ready? What is the temperature of the melt?"

"The men are here and ready, sir. I took the temperature myself with the pyrometer just ten minutes ago. It is stable at one thousand four hundred degrees Celsius."

"Very well, then, tell the men to move the mold into position next to the caudron. Seal the doors and instruct the men to get into their shielded suits for the pour."

"Very well, sir. Thank you," said Ali, and turned to do so.

Dr. Ferreydoon thought to himself that it would be a good thing if they could film the actual pour for historical preservation, but his instructions were to pour the core in utmost secrecy. They could film another pour later and pretend that it was the original pour for filming, anyway.

Ali and his crew had moved the mold into position on the terrazzo floor next to the cauldron. The cauldron was suspended in a cradle and pivoted on bearings on each side. The supports that reached up from the carriage on each side of the cauldron supported the cauldron so that it could be tilted to load it or to pour its liquefied metal contents into ingot molds, or, in this case, into the mold for the weapon's core. This was a solemn and joyful moment for the entire crew. As Dr. Ferreydoon approached, they all knelt and prayed.

Once their prayers were completed, Dr. Ferreydoon moved to the carriage and got the control from its hook and backed up to the extent the cable would allow from the cauldron. The heat was intense even with the efficient exhaust fans. He looked around at the apprehensive faces of his men. Ali nodded to Dr.Ferreydoon and Ferreydoon pushed and held down the button that caused the huge cauldron to tilt in its cradle. It took all of fifteen seconds for the cauldron to tilt enough for the first shower of liquid metal to come from the lip of the cauldron. Another ten seconds and they were getting enough flow, so he stopped the tilting action and waited. It took about three minutes for the mold to fill. When it seemed that it was close to full, Dr. Ferredoon began to tilt the cauldron back to a vertical position. As the mold filled, the extra metal began to fill the sprue outside the mold. That part would be cut off and shaped with hand tools to the same contour as the main body of the core and the extra metal would be put back into the cauldron for the next pour. Once they had completed the pour, Dr.Ferreydoon tripped the switch to cut power to the heating unit and the cauldron would begin to cool back down to room temperature. It would take about thirteen hours for it to come down, even with the ventilating fans on their highest setting.

He directed the men to move the mold, which was on a carriage of its own, away from the cauldron to its place in the far corner of the lab where it would cool for about eight hours before they could cut off the spue and reshape the core.

Dr. Ferreydoon assembled the men after they had moved the core to the far corner of the lab. He told them that they had achieved a milestone event and that he was very proud of them. He said that he would go to his office and write up his report of this morning's activities. He said he was very proud of them, but cautioned them that they were to behave as if nothing unusual had occurred when they talked with other workers here underground. They nodded their agreement and the group dispersed.

Dr. Ferreydoon walked out of the lab and down the hall to his office. As he walked, he felt the temperature of his garments lower and by the time he got to his office, he felt that his clothing was back to normal temperature. He picked up the mike for his dictating machine and began to recount his activities and those of his men on this historic morning.

Chapter 18

Lero and Jean had met at her workshop and lab for lunch and to talk about the project. He said, "I have been thinking about the actual strike for some time. My belief is that we should strike where the trigger may be assembled onto the device, whether that is at another facility than where it has been built or at the test site itself. That means that we only have to choose the assembly site correctly and the test site. There are only a few places where I believe there is enough technical help and security for this.

He rolled out their large planning chart with the nuclear sites and other places of interest clearly marked. The chart was three feet wide and four feet tall. The table was about forty inches high, just right for working on avionics and the other mechanisms they used in "the enterprise." He had turned to get a magnifying glass from his kit and she bent over to smooth a corner of the chart. When he turned around she was leaning over the table in just such a way that it reminded him of the times when she needed him to help her apply her all-over moisturizer lotion. He impulsively slipped his right arm around her waist and pulled her to him firmly. She gasped nicely and whispered, "Oh, I love it when you pull me to you that way."

"Me, too," he whispered into her right ear.

He kissed her exposed neck very artfully and they were lost to other thoughts,

Jean whispered, "I am glad I latched the door after you came in. Do you want me to get the lights."

"No, the sight of you is so exciting, and I don't want to let go of you for that long."

Chapter 19

An hour and a half later, as they had lunch in the white Grand Cherokee at Sonic, she brought up the subject of the nuclear sites again. She was feeding him a French fry so he did not have to remove his right hand from her left breast. He loved that she did not wear underwear to their lunches after encounters. The tinted windows of the Cherokee gave them confidence in their privacy.

"If we station one man at each facility you suspect, in a position to use a laser designator, how many would that be?"

"I think we can narrow the list to six facilities. We still don't know where they will conduct the test, so we should add another two or three to the list to cover those sites, too."

She looked at him with an affectionate gaze, then she reached over and gave him a sweet kiss. He was glad he had not taken his hand from her breast. He had asked her to drive so he could devote appropriate attention to fondling her during lunch.

As she drew up to him about six inches from his face, she whispered, "I love you, Dan."

He whispered, "I love you, too," just before their lips met.

A few minutes later, she asked, "Don't you think we should be discussing the project?"

He said, "Well, Okay, provided I don't have to let go of you."

She giggled in a sweet, personal way.

"My favorite facility for the assembly is Natanz. It is huge and they could find any one of several places there to secretly assemble the device. My second favorite is Parchin. What do you think?" he asked.

"Well, if it is Natanz, its protection with concrete and rocks and soil will make it very difficult to strike it in such a way as to destroy the trigger and not trigger a nuclear blast AND make it look like an accident. I think it would be pretty obvious to their investigators that the blast originated externally," she said.

"I agree," he said. "That is going to be very challenging. It would be much easier to deceive them if the assembly takes place at Parchin. I sure hope we get some inside information. Guessing where this will take place is so imprecise. We could easily miss the whole thing with an incorrect choice. How are you coming along with the telemetry and encoding?

"Oh, fine," she said. "Ernie and I have pretty well worked out the details of a protocol to awaken the module and activate it. One thing we are not sure of is which tubes have which kind of weapon. We want to be sure to use a high explosive warhead and not a nuke."

"Wow. Sure thing," said Lero. "Let me know as soon as you figure that out, if you do."

"Okay," she said and slipped him another French fry.

"I would much rather we destroy the trigger during transport and make it look like it blew up spontaneously," he said. "I can visualize them coming to that conclusion if there were only a smoking hole in the ground."

"Hitting a moving target would be challenging, but feasible, especially if it does not change speed during the last few seconds of the missile's flight," she said. "The technology of the guidance system is rather primitive, but I think we can be confident of a strike within fifty feet of any point."

"That is close enough," he said. "If the target is stationary, could be strike with more precision?"

"Yes, Ernie and I are pretty confident that a stationary target can be hit within ten feet."

"I have to confess, sometimes the enormity of what we are doing is overwhelming. Just think of the devastation if we choose the wrong weapon. It is scary," she said. "The time of flight of the missile is a challenge, too. I sometimes wish the weapons were in a lower orbit, geostationary, or not. The flight time would be a few minutes instead of an hour."

"I understand," he said. "If they were not assembling a nuclear device and if they had no such recent history of heated rhetoric and actual military action, it would make me question whether the strike were a good idea. This could kill tens of thousands of people and devastate an entire area if we mess up. I don't have many qualms about hitting people who are one or two steps from hitting us or our friends, but I would have serious reservations about a strike if there were not such a clear threat to us and our friends."

"I am not trying to duck our responsibility here. But, we have to realize that we have a moral responsibility to speak up if our leadership asks us to do something that we feel is morally wrong," she said. "Do you believe that Mr. Murfree and his associates actually realize the risk here?"

"I am very confident that they appreciate the risk. The political implications of this situation are enormous. I have no doubt that there are multiple factors at work that we don't know about and that they intend it to be that way. Our job is to focus on getting this thing to work correctly at the appropriate time and get our field people in position to achieve that as quickly as possible."

"When we get back to the office, I need to call Rusty to see how he stands with filling the roster."

"I guess we need to get back, but I hate the idea of you taking your hand off of me. I fit in your hand so nicely," she said.

"I would have described it exactly like that, too," he said. They shared a look. They could not resist one more lingering kiss before she started the Cherokee.

Chapter 20

Ali knocked at the door of Dr. Ferreydoon's office.

"Yes. Come in," he said.

Ali said, "Doctor, we have completed the cutting of the sprue and the reshaping of the core. It is ready for your inspection."

"Good," said Ferreydoon. "I will be down directly."

In ten minutes, Dr. Ferreydoon entered the lab and approached the men gathered around the fabrication table. On the table, wrapped in a lead sheath, was the core that they had poured three days before, now with its mold sprue cut off and nicely reshaped to the contour of the rest of the core. It had been wire brushed all over, so that one could not tell where the sprue had been. He looked in over carefully and smiled at his men.

"This is superb. I wish we could show this off, but secrecy demands that we keep it here covered up. You men have done a fine job. You may now transport it to the assembly bay and put it in the device. Do so under utmost secrecy. I would prefer that you transport it on the rubber tired cart at a time when the fewest people will be working at any place between here and the assembly bay. Ali, please let me know when you are ready to transport, as I want to attend," said Dr.Ferreydoon.

He walked back to his office to dictate his progress notes for the morning.

"Won't be long now," he thought as he strolled the long corridor.

Chapter 21

Professor Ferrydoon took the call in his office, just off the main chamber of the laboratory. No secretary answered for him. He simply said, "Hello."

A voice on the other end said, "Transport today to Parchin. Assist assembly. Once assembled, transport to Site Y."

Very well. Allah U Akbar," said Ferrydoon.

"Zila, I will need you to help me take a heavy package to my car."

"Surely, Professor Ferrydoon. I will get the cart."

The two of them loaded the "package" into a padded case and flipped the latches downward to latch the two halves of the case together. With the "package" in it, the case weighted about one hundred twenty pounds. They used the overhead crane to lift the package onto the wheeled cart and then moved the crane back into its stored position in the corner of the room.

Zila opened the door for the Professor and together they wheeled the cart down a long corridor to a pair of metal double doors. Outside the doors was a loading dock. He had pulled his Toyota Land Cruiser into the loading dock and backed it up near to the edge. Together, they lifted the case off of the cart and onto the dock. Then they moved the cart back. Professor Ferrydoon went down the two steps to the garage floor and helped Zila push the case over to the edge of the loading dock. Then she came down to the floor and they picked up each end of the case by its handles and manhandled it into the open trunk of the car. With the rear seats folded down, it went in easily with plenty of room to spare.

While Ferrydoon closed the trunk lid, Zila moved to the driver's side door to hold it for Ferrydoon. While he was occupied, she slipped a TracPhone into the side pocket of the door.

She stood back as Ferrydoon came forward and got into the car.

"I will be gone for a few days. Watch over things until I get back," he said.

"Of course," she said as he closed the door and started the car.

She did not wait to watch him out of sight, but went back to the office as soon as the car began to move. She went back into the laboratory and resumed her position at her desk. She took out another TracPhone from a desk drawer and retrieved a slip of paper from her underclothes. She dialed the number on the slip of paper and let it ring several times. Then she hung up and took the phone with her into the restroom. There, in a stall, she took the battery out of the phone and broke it apart where it hinged and flushed the pieces down the toilet.

When she got back to the office, she took out another Trac phone and dialed a number she knew by heart. She did not realize it, but the telephone called a repeater about a mile and a half from her office. It relayed the conversation onto a satellite link. She was actually talking with the duty officer at Dalgren Air Force Base at Wallops Island, Virginia. The voice on the other end answered on the fourth ring.

"Hello."

She said, "Ninety percent probability either Natanz or Parchin. White Toyota Land Cruiser. Driver only. Left about ten minutes ago. End of message."

There was a click on the other end as the duty officer hung up. Since she was alone in her room, no one thought it strange that she visited the ladies room again so soon after the earlier trip. She went into a stall and dismantled the Trac phone like she had done to the earlier one and flushed the components down the toilet. She had done all she could. Now it was up to someone else to follow through.

She worked the rest of the day drafting reports of his recorded observations and his meticulous notes from the assembly of the trigger. She put print outs of the reports into his journal and put the journal on her desk on the left corner like he instructed her to do and like she did at the close of each day.

When the end of her shift arrived, she rose from her desk, went to the coat rack in the corner and retrieved her chador, which she carefully wrapped around herself. As she paused at the door to turn off the lights, she looked back into the laboratory where she had worked for the last two years and realized that she was leaving it for the last time. She tripped the switch to turn off the lights and closed the door, and walked down the long corridor to the door that led to the outside.

She caught the street car as usual. She used her own cell phone to make a short call as she watched the northern part of Tehran pass by through the dirty windows. She was back in her apartment in an hour.

She packed a small suitcase with only those most necessary items. Just enough fresh clothes for a couple of days, the usual toiletries and an extra pair of shoes. She put in a man's jacket and cap and closed the lid. She left all of her other personal items. She dressed in loose fitting man's slacks and a man's shirt. A man's chafiya topped off the ensemble. The pattern would tell anyone who knew anything that she (masquerading as a he) was a Kurd. Without makeup, she could pass for a guy if someone did not look too closely.

After dark, she sat by the window waiting for the car to pull up. When it did, she grabbed the suitcase, took one more look around and went out the door. As she approached, the driver reached over and pushed the passenger side door open. She pulled the suitcase up in front of her and got into the car in one fluid motion. As she shut the door, the driver moved away. She did not look back.

This was her chance to go to the west. She had been hoping and planning for three years. Now, that chance was mixed with the danger of what she had done. She knew that once the "event" took place, if it did, the Revolutionary Guard would be backtracking. Even if they found the phone, they could not tie it to her. She even took the precaution of wiping it off carefully before Dr.

Ferrydoon came back to the lab. She had gloves on while she was handling the case with him, too.

Now, she knew that it was just a matter of getting out. She knew that her contact would do his best to get her out and that he had powerful friends. Her friend dropped her off at the bus station on the southwest side of Tehran. She bought a ticket for Mashhad, near the Turkministan and Afghan borders, but intended to leave the bus before it arrived there. The bus did not leave for an hour and a half. She leaned against her duffel bag at the end of a bench in the corner and took a nap.

She dreamed of meeting a kind, gentle man somewhere in the west, a man who would appreciate her and be good to her and fill her belly with their babies.

Shortly after the appointed time, the old bus lumbered up to the loading area after the driver had checked it over, wiped its windshield, and filled the tank with diesel fuel. The canned announcement, in a lady's voice announced the bus and the other cities it would go to on its trip. She waited until a line had formed, then swung her duffel on her shoulder and got in line. The clerk who punched her ticket did not really look at her as she boarded. She found a window seat near the rear of the bus and settled in for a long night's ride. The bus had the ambience of unwashed bodies and the faint aroma of goats. In about five minutes, the driver pulled the lever next to his seat to pull the door closed and they were under way.

She thought about how wonderful it felt to be going, at last, to a new life. She knew it would not be easy, but she was convinced that it held wonderful potential. Those thoughts mixed with the dread she felt when she thought about what they would do to her if she did not make it across the border. As she tossed with the other passengers when the bus negotiated the bumpy, curvy roads over the mountains east of Tehran, she could not go to sleep until deep into the night.

At the stop at Semnan, about a hundred fifty kilometers east of Tehran, she went into the station with the rest of the passengers. Like most, she headed directly for the toilet. She came out of the toilet, intending to get right back on the bus, but the old lady behind the bar in the restaurant section of the bus station was stirring a large pot of something that smelled delicious, so she walked over and bought a bowl of lamb stew and a half a loaf of naan. She sat, like the others, on the crude bench in the middle of the station and eagerly ate the stew and naan. When she had finished, she threw the paper bowl and plastic spoon in the trash can and opened a bottle of water to finish off her meal. It was colder up in the mountains and it was after two in the morning. The temperature had dropped into the forties and she shrugged her coat close to herself as she walked back to the bus. She sat and ate an apple as the bus pulled out into the night.

Chapter 22

In the darkened cabin of the AWACS, forty one thousand feet over western Afghanistan, Staff Sergeant Melody Griffis keyed the mike in her headset with the button on her computer mouse. "Captain, you better come and see this," she said.

Captain Orvil Butler walked back down the aisle of the AWACs aircraft between the consoles to where Griffis was seated.

"What've you got?" he asked as he looked over her shoulder at the screen.

"You told us to be alert for a particular cell telephone in zone fifty four. I have got a signal."

"He squinted at the screen closely and said: "Good catch, Sergeant. I'll be back in a minute."

He hurried to his console at the front of the compartment. He put on his headset and turned the dial of his communications radio to a discrete frequency. He could hear the click as the satellite circuit closed.

"Good evening," was the only greeting on the other end.

"This is Captain Butler on station in AWACS three thirteen. Tell your party that we are picking up the carrier broadcast from the cell phone he was curious about and it is moving."

"Will do," said the voice. "Maintain contact if possible. Stay on this frequency and continue to observe and report location and direction and speed every five minutes."

"Yes, sir," said Butler.

He pushed another button on his console and said into his headset: "Griffis, I am going to patch you to a satellite circuit. Report the location, direction and speed of the cell phone every five minutes until orders change."

"Yes, Captain," said Griffis as she leaned closer to the screen at her console. The moving map display on her screen showed the signal moving southwesterly from Tehran, nearing the Zagros mountains. It was averaging about fifty kilometers per hour.

Chapter 23

Lero was standing in the kitchen, holding a bowl of cereal in one hand and a spoon in the other, watching the morning news on the satellite broadcast when his cell phone vibrated on the counter. He put down the bowl and spoon and answered.

"Hello," he said.

"Mr. Murfree advises that the hen is on the nest and the chicken is crossing the road."

"Thank you, message received and understood," said Lero and both parties hung up. Jean walked in the kitchen just as he hung up the phone.

"Things are moving," he said. "I need to take you back to Tempe. You had better pack for a week or so. I will be leaving from here this evening on a shuttle flight to get closer to Disneyland."

"I know this is serious and we will be working halfway around the world from each other for Gosh who knows how long. Do you think we could spare a moment to help me with something in the bedroom?" she asked with a sweet wide eyed innocent look.

"Of course," he said. "Show me what you need help with."

Later in the morning, as he packed the few things at the office that he would need on his trip, the satellite phone on his desk vibrated.

"Hold for Mr. Murfree, please."

After a pause, the familiar voice came on. "Say the word please."

"Houston."

"I am going to send you an encrypted file with the latest on their movements and the analyses of our best people about the intentions and geographical references. I am glad you are leaving presently. The B-1 will have you to Prince Sultan in six hours. Keep me advised about your plans. Thanks for doing this for us. God be with you."

"Thank you, sir. Talk to you soon."

Lero checked his email and found the encrypted file. He opened and, after reading the cautionary preface, keyed the computer to print the entire file. As the printer was doing its job, he put the last of his equipment into his brain bag for the trip.

As the printer finished printing the encrypted file, he walked over and removed the sheets from the printer and estimated them at forty pages. He slipped them into a manila envelope and put it in the bag.

Velma called on the intercom and said, "Air traffic control advises your transport will be available in forty five minutes."

"Thanks, Velma," he said into the intercom. "Come in please."

She stepped in with her note pad at the ready, an old and good habit.

"I will be out of the office for a few days. Call me on the satellite phone any time you think a message needs forwarding. Jean is working at a remote location, but can be reached by cell phone or satellite phone any time. We are in constant contact. Thank you, Velma. I really appreciate you and how well you run this place."

Velma sensed that there was something big afoot. Lero always was appreciative of her efforts, but this time, he seemed a little tense about the trip he was going on.

She said, "I will take care of the home fires. You just take care of yourself."

She turned to leave, but hesitated at the office door and turned to say, "I am so glad you and Jean found each other. Does she know where you are going?"

"Yes, she does, Velma. Thanks."

Velma was ten years older than Lero and treated him like her younger brother. She had been a fixture at the unit since Jefe brought her with him from Arlington. They had worked together for more than twenty five years.

Chapter 24

In the remote Zagros Mountains about 195 kilometers southeast of Esfahan, stood the deserted Tungsten mine operated in the seventies by the French Conglomerate Bezancon Companie. The entrance is on west slope at about four thousand feet MSL. The main tunnel is eight feet high for most of its length to allow passage of rail cars bringing ore out of the mine. The main drift tunnel extends easterly into the mountain for three thousand five hundred meters. The opening was sealed with a two meter thick concrete plug when Bezancon ceased operations. That has been removed and a new false façade has been built in front of the entrance, allowing entry of vehicles as wide as two and a half meters. The façade is covered with rock and dirt from the surrounding area. A vehicle entering must make a right angle turn to enter the tunnel, but from outside, it is very difficult to see where the tunnel actually is.

The chart on the Situation Room table was between the President and the briefer, Admiral Shalikash.

"With a moderately high level of confidence, we believe that the agency in charge of developing a nuclear device has up-fitted the Hekmat Nine site in preparation for an underground nuclear test. The alternate plan is that if we cannot interdict the trigger in transit to Hekmat Nine, we will strike it with a low yield nuclear device as shortly after it is delivered to the mine as we can, hoping that it will be interpreted as a botched test and an accidental detonation of the nuclear device. On the other hand, it we strike the vehicle transporting the trigger to the mine, the elves are soon going to figure out that it was a hostile act. In either case, the loss of the trigger without having determined if it worked properly and the loss of key personnel at the blast site will set them back at least a year, we believe."

"Very well, Admiral. Keep me informed, please. I think this is coming together."

"Yes, sir," said the Admiral and stepped back so the President could leave the briefing room.

Chapter 25

Sergeant Major Hopkins took the call himself, since he rotated the watch duty with his men. It was about three AM local time. Only about a fifth of the men on duty at the Forward Operating base were awake at the time.

The satellite phone was set to a low ring tone. It startled him because it rang so seldom and rarely in the middle of the night watch.

"Forward Operating Base Kilo Thirteen, Sergeant Major Hopkins speaking," he said into the telephone headset.

"Sergeant Major Hopkins, this is Colonel Graham at CentCom."

"Yes, sir, Colonel Graham, what can I do for you?" said Hopkins.

"We need an extraction helicopter and team to go into Iran and extract an agent before the bad guys catch up with her. She is riding a bus that left Tehran last evening at eight. She is scheduled to arrive at Mashhad in about three hours. Our sources have told us that the authorities are waiting at the bus station in Mashhad to take her into custody. If they do that it will cause a major flap. We want you to intercept the bus with a crew of special operators and get her out of there before the bus reaches Mashhad. We roughly calculate the distance from you to Mashhad is one hundred eighty clicks. The intercept should take place in the foothills west of Mashhad. We would prefer that the bus passengers not see or hear the helo. The bus is a Hino, probably manufactured in two thousand two. Light gray color. Number on sides of bus and top is eight five two. We believe that operators in native dress with Kalishnikovs and RPG launchers should make it appear as a bandit attack. I will be sending a picture and a bio by email in the next five minutes. If you do not receive it, notify us. We will update you as to location of the bus from AWACS on a frequency sent to you in the email. We place all the tactical decisions in your hands. Use your best judgment. Report to us by relay from AWACS on the frequency two forty six decimal seven megahertz. Do you have all that?"

"Yes, sir, said Hopkins. "If I may ask, sir, what is the priority level of the package we are to ex-filtrate?"

"She is priority level five, Sergeant Major. She has a pharmaceutical pack and knows how to use it in case her capture is imminent. Please don't let her be captured alive, Sergeant Major."

There was a pause, then Hopkins said, "Understood, sir. We will give it our best effort. Thank you for your confidence in us, sir."

"The radio call sign of the AWACS is Centaur Five. Your call sign is Reggio One. Bring all your men back safe and your package, too, Sergeant Major. Good luck."

"Whew," said the Sergeant Major to himself. With his left hand, he pushed a button that instantly connected his headset to all of the shoulder radios on the base and to all of the speakers in the buildings.

"Attention: this is Sergeant Major Hopkins. Alert! Alert! We have an urgent mission. I need two helo crews for a mission on the pad in ten minutes. I need ground crews to prepare two helos for a maximum range flight. I need two teams of six men combat ready to man the helos. Dress and weapons will be local. Report to the helo pads in ten minutes. Briefing for all involved personnel will take place on the helo pad. Move!"

Forward Operating Base Kilo Thirteen came alive. The sounds of men running could be heard from Hopkins' desk within seconds of his alert message. He grabbed up a map of the part of Iran that lay to the west of Kilo Thirteen, a flashlight and his helmet. There were one hundred sixty four men on base. All were awake now. He walked out the door of his office tent and toward the helo pads. The fuel trucks were just finishing topping off the tanks of the two Blackhawks when he stepped onto the pierced steel padding that formed the base of the pad. The trucks finished their work and moved off.   Men began to arrive from all directions, it seemed. In ten minutes, the troops were assembled beside the nearest one. Hopkins walked up to the group and they came to attention.

"At ease, men," he said. "We have something important tonight. You men will leave here with lights out, proceed about forty clicks west of the town of Mashhad, Iran, about one hundred clicks from here. You will land where the helos cannot be observed from the road. I have marked a suggested location on the maps to be provided to your pilots. Use another landing site at your discretion. You will intercept a civilian commercial bus, number 852, that is on its way to Mashhad, ex-filtrate a female passenger whom you will identify by a picture and by her name, pretend that is it a kidnapping to cover the true purpose of the exfiltration, then let the other passengers and driver go, bring her back here and do not fire a shot unless you have to. Use your judgment. This passenger is a high priority package. Exercise appropriate care. Pilots and air crew be advised, we will position a refueling blivet about fifty clicks east of Mashhad in case you run low on fuel on the return trip. Call sign will be given you by radio. Time is of the essence. Get moving. Address all questions to me on the scrambled radio after departure. Come back safely, men. God be with you. That is all."

Hopkins gave each squad leader a package with a picture of Zila and a short bio on her. He watched as the men piled into the Blackhawks. Rotors began to rotate, then to spin. Dust flew as the pilots powered up. In a short time, both helos lifted off almost simultaneously. In five minutes they were over the ridge to the west. Hopkins stood on the helo pad and said a prayer for his men and the mission. He noted the time: Three twenty three local, and wrote it down. Then he slowly walked back to his watch station.

Zila was awakened from a fitful sleep by the sudden deceleration of the bus. She was almost pulled forward out of her seat by it. By the time she recovered enough to sit up in the seat, she looked out the side window and saw a group of armed men standing in the lights of the bus. The driver told everyone to remain in their seats. A man approached the door and the driver opened it. The man climbed into the bus and, without a word, started down the aisle with his Kalishnikov held at the ready. As soon as he got a few feet down the aisle, a second man, armed likewise, stepped in and stayed near the driver at the front of the bus. He looked at each passenger carefully. When he got to Zila, he stopped and said in Farsi, "Come with me."

She recoiled in terror and shook her head "No." He could see she was terrified, so he held up a card that had printed on it, also in Farsi "I am an American Soldier. Come with me, Zila." She burst into tears. The casual onlooker would have thought that they were tears fear and dread, but they were tears of joy. She grabbed up her duffel and walked slowly back down the aisle of the bus to the front. The driver gave her a look of helplessness and she nodded to him as if to say, "It's alright, I understand." She stepped out of the bus and took a couple of steps and turned back to look at it. The man who came for her motioned to the driver to go on, and the bus lurched ahead. In minute, it was out of sight and earshot over a low ridge.

The man next to her, took off his chafiya and said to her in English: "Sorry to have frightened you that way. Come with us. You are safe now."

She said earnestly, "Thank you, thank you."

The group of men and Zila began to walk down the road in the direction from which the bus had come. About a hundred yards back, they left the road and walked about another two hundred yards into the brush and scrub trees. They soon came to a small clearing where two menacing looking helicopters sat silently. As they walked up, a crewman opened the door of the closest one and hopped down onto the dusty soil. He reached for Zila's duffel and gently tossed it up onto the deck of the passenger compartment. The other crewman had put down a ladder for her to climb up, which she did without hesitation. The others silently followed her. Once on board, the lead took a count of his men and gave a thumbs up sign to the pilot who was watching expectantly from the flight deck. When he saw the sign, he hit the start button and held it in. Mechanical things began to happen and a whine filled the helo, making conversation impossible without a headset. The crewman offered Zila a headset so she could hear what was being said by the pilots and crew. In about a minute, the two pilots nodded to each other and then turned to the front. Almost immediately the power increased and dust flew all around. The two helos lifted off in tandem and climbed into the night. They started east as they climbed, toward Forward Operating Base Kilo Thirteen. The only lights visible were on the panel ahead of the pilots.

Chapter 26

The phone on Lero's desk rang. He was reading a report from an operative that had been dictated by satellite phone the night before. He put down the report and picked up the phone. It was the phone that he answered only "Hello," not the normal office phone that Velma would answer for normal business.

"Hello," he said.

The male voice on the other end just said in an unexcited way, "Hold please for Mr. Murfree."

Lero did not respond aloud, but held.

In a moment, the familiar voice of Mr. Murfree came on. "Hello, say the word, please."

Lero said, "Houston."

Then they both knew whom they were talking to.

"We have missed our chance to hit the trigger before transport to the assembly facility. It left in Professor Ferrydoon's Toyota Land Cruiser forty minutes ago. We think it is on its way to the Natanz facility, but it may be another site. The distance to the Natanz facility is over four hundred kilometers, so we have some time to act if we are able before it goes underground. Our AWACS on station in western Afghanistan is trailing the car with the package. What is your state of readiness?"

Lero said, "Ernie and Jean have worked out the operational protocols and are ready to act, but there has not been enough time for our guys on the ground to get into position. We estimate that will take another twenty four hours or so."

"Okay," said the President. "Get them into position to launch as soon as possible. Report to me on this phone when they are ready to act. Get me a detailed report of the whereabouts of our men and their readiness as soon as you can, hopefully within the hour and call me back."

"Yes, sir. Thanks," said Lero and they hung up.

Now, the fat was in the fire. He called Jean on his cell phone. She answered on the second ring.

"Hi," what is up?" she asked.

"The chicken is crossing the road," he said. "Mr. Murfree wants you and Ernie ready to function as soon as possible, and stand by for a "go" order. I think the fastest way is for me to pick you up and drive to Tempe. Call him and alert him that we are enroute and let him know that we may need to act promptly. See you in a minute."

"Sure thing, see you then," she said and hung up.

By the time he got to the building where her lab was located, she was standing in the parking lot with her brief case.

When he stopped, she put the briefcase in the back seat and climbed in, fastening her seat belt even before she reached over and kissed him.

"Well, here we go," she said, and settled into the leather seat.

It was seventy five miles to Ernie's building on the campus of Arizona State. They made it in less than an hour. Lero drove the desert highways at about eighty five, with the high beam headlights on, as is the custom on the desert highways.

Chapter 27

Rusty answered on the third ring. There was a lot of background noise because he was in a Chinook helicopter with troops.

The National Reconnaissance Office was busy. They were monitoring several sites of interest at the same time. Consoles with operators were arranged in a "U" shape in a room with subdued lighting. Air Force Sergeant Dorothy Stanton sat at one of the consoles near the closed end of the "U." She was watching a small opening in a rocky landscape. To the casual observer, it looked like a large version of a garage door, set in a cliff face. It was painted to match the surrounding terrain. There were barely visible tracks outside the door in the sand that blew constantly across that region. No pavement led from the opening, but information provided said that the area outside of the opening was firm rocky ground, and, contrary to its appearance, it had been carefully prepared so it could accept the largest vehicles that might potentially be used within. Her orders were to report any entering or exiting vehicle to the watch commander, who would then assign each exiting vehicle to an analyst to follow. Suspicion was that the exiting vehicle they were anticipating would be a large truck, probably one with double axles in the rear, because of the weight of the "package" being transported, and to disguise the contents by putting the truck into the normal flow of trucks that came and went from the site. Even though the door was painted to match the surrounding terrain, using the infrared filter, they could clearly see that it was a "foreign material, probably metal" when they first detected it on the east face of a mountain side west of Natanz, Iran. Now, it was a well known item and was under constant surveillance. She had not been told what was afoot, but only to report vehicles leaving. The watch officer did not know the reason for the order particularly requesting information on all vehicles leaving the site, either. No need to know.

Chapter 28

The Grand Ayatollah was enjoying the late afternoon on a balcony adjacent to his office. His aide stepped to the door and in a low voice, said, "Your Highness, General Askani is here."

"Very well. Show him in," said the Grand Ayatollah.

In a moment, General Askani stepped up to the chair where the Grand Ayatollah was sitting, facing away from the door, where he could survey the expanse of Tehran.

"Greetings, your majesty. You sent for me?" asked the General.

"Yes. Have a seat, please."

"Thank you, sir," said the general.

"First of all, congratulations on your recent achievement, mating the trigger to the device. I understand your people worked tirelessly on it and that it is now ready to be tested."

"Yes, majesty. Our people are very dedicated. You are correct. The device is now ready to be tested."

"Rather than place it on a ship and take it to a remote area of the Indian Ocean for testing, I would prefer that you test it underground."

"Yes, majesty," said the general.

"For secrecy's sake, I want you to choose a site in the central desert where there are plenty of old worked out mines. Place the device far enough below ground so detection of the blast by the international community of watchers will only be able to determine a general area, not a specific site. Do not attempt to tell me where the device is to be detonated. I am very concerned about secrecy and the attempt to inform me may be intercepted. You will not communicate with me again unless there is some reason to postpone or cancel the test. Pick the time of the test yourself, General. Observe utmost secrecy. I will be able to tell that you have performed the test by watching the American television broadcasts by satellite. They will react almost immediately. After the test, come back to report to me, and me only, about the test.

"It shall be done as you direct, majesty," said Askani

"Very well. May Allah guide you and keep you," said the Grand Ayatollah.

Askari stood and saluted and then turned and left the balcony. The Grand Ayatollah resumed his solitary thoughts about the revolution in the setting sunlight.

"How are we ever going to get a team into Disneyland in time to interdict the device before Professor Ferrydoon gets it to the assembly site or the test site?" Jean asked.

"We don't have anyone close enough and we don't have the means to get anyone close enough in time," said Lero.

"If you are correct that the assembly will take place at Parchin or Natanz, how long will it take for him to get to either place?"

"I estimate it will take him six hours to reach Parchin and eight and a half hours to get to Natanz, at normal speeds. There is no way we can hit the trigger before it gets to where it is being transported now. What we need to do is determine where it went and devise a plan to hit it where it is or enroute or at the test site. We can plan to hit it at Natanz, or at Parchin, or on its way to the test site, wherever that may be, assuming we detect the transporting vehicle or vehicles and can follow them."

General Askani got out of his comfortable car into the stifling heat of the central desert. Colonel Fusin stepped up and saluted.

"This is the mine I was telling you about, General. Would you like to go with me to have a look?"

"Yes, indeed. Let's have a closer look," said Askani.

"My technician, Major Saleh, proposed this mine," General. "He has had his squad of men looking urgently for several days."

Chapter 29

The satellite phone beside Lero's bunk rang softly. He awakened on the second ring. He reached out and pulled it over next to him.

"Hello," he said.

"Hold for Mr. Murfree," the voice said.

In a moment, the familiar voice of the President came on.

"Say the word, please."

Lero said, "Houston."

"What is your twenty?" asked the President.

"Sir, I am at Prince Sultan Air Base in Saudi Arabia."

"I just wanted to let you know that we will have to change plans. We may not have time enough to get teams of men into Disneyland. Our information is that the egg is on the roll now and should reach the first roost by later this evening. I want you to coordinate with Major Ames at the National Reconnaissance Office to complete your planning. The first option is no longer available to us. We will need to try to put something together to respond to the second contingency. Failing that, we will need to decide if we want to go to Plan three.

"Alright, sir," said Lero. "I will get on it immediately. Sorry we could not hit the chicken on its first attempt to cross the road."

"Not to worry," said Mr. Murfree. "We were not up to speed in time. No one's fault. Just let me know what you guys plan and keep me in the loop with periodic reports, please."

"Will do, sir. How long do your people estimate it will take them to graft the chicken to the egg?"

"Our people estimate at least a day, maybe two."

"Good. That gives us a little time to fill out a dance card. I will get back with you once we have a menu for the dinner."

"Good. Sorry I awakened you. When did you get to Prince Sultan?"

"I arrived on the B-1 about three hours ago, sir."

"I see. Well, get some rest when you can, but let me hear from you as soon as you have some thoughts about the menu."

"Will do, sir. Good night."

"Good night,"

Mr. Murfree rang off. The phone gave an audible click.

Chapter 30

Lero got out his contact book and found the number for the duty desk at the NRO. The phone rang twice before a female voice answered.

"Major MacInnis," she said.

"This is Lero. May I speak to Major Ames, please."

"Certainly, sir. Just hold, please."

In a short moment, Major Ames came on and identified himself.

"Glad to hear from you so promptly. What is your twenty?"

"Prince Sultan Air Base," said Lero.

"Good. We are trailing three vehicles now that meet the description given to us. Our most likely vehicle is about thirty miles west of Esfahan, approaching Natanz. I expect it to reach Natanz in about forty minutes. Once it goes underground, we will not know what kind of vehicle to expect for the second stage of transport. We must be very vigilant. What is your belief about a vehicle?" he asked.

"I would pick a two and a half ton truck, by itself. Mixed in with the normal traffic to throw off suspicion."

"That is a good idea. I will alert our technicians to be on the lookout for one. We log every outgoing vehicle, anyway. Do you want us to report to you all vehicles that exit?"

"Not for a while. It will take them about one or two days to accomplish what we suspect they are doing. Start really concentrating a day from now and let me know all traffic, please, on this number."

"Will do, sir. Thank you."

"Thank you guys, too. I know this is an unusual request, but it is worth the effort."

"G-2 called and said to give it top priority. I will have my best people on this around the clock. Call me if you have any questions, please."

"Will do, and thanks again, Major Ames."

"You are welcome. Good luck," said Ames.

Next, Lero dialed a number he knew well. On the fifth ring, Jefe answered, his voice heavy with sleep.

"Hey, there," said Lero. "Sorry to wake you, but I need to get the word to you so you can pass it along. Phase one is no longer a viable option. The transport is almost completed. We need to have our invitees ready for the party for the second dance or maybe the third. Where are your guys now?"

There was a pause while Jefe determined his local time, then thought a bit.

"Over the Atlantic about an hour west of Gibraltar. Should reach you in about three or four hours. Shall I pass along that the first dance is over?"

"No, I can tell them when they get here. The fewer transmissions the better. Face to face on this one is better."

"Well, okay. Let me know if I can do anything."

"Sure enough. Thanks for getting the gang together. I will let you know what we need. Thanks for being there."

"You are welcome. Be careful."

Chapter 31

"Will do, thanks." They hung up.

Next, Lero dialed Jean's number. She answered on the second ring. After a moment for a personal greeting, Lero asked Jean, "Do you know how closely the birds can be expected to have the same velocity? I am thinking of having a wake up call before the party."

"No, I will have to ask Ernie. Are you thinking of a pair?"

"Yes, a firecracker followed by big brother."

"I will ask him and let you know. Be careful with yourself. I miss you."

"I miss you, too. See you soon. Bye."

"Bye," she said and hung up.

When she put the question to Ernie, he said he would have to study and think about the answer and get back. He said it would take an hour or two.

Jean was in her lab/shop when Ernie called back.

"The noses are different shapes and the weight is different. The engines are similar. Allowing for the absence of drag out there, I think there might be as much as four or five percent difference in rate. With a commuting time of about an hour, I would advise sending the first down the road a good five minutes before number two. Is our friend thinking of hitting two places at once?"

"No, he is thinking of consecutive events and wants the popcorn before the movie."

"I think that is an excellent idea. We could use the popcorn to make the way for the movie. It might be interpreted as an unfortunate result that caused the movie to play."

"Things are heating up," she said. "I will need to come to your place and camp out for a while."

"We have a bunk for you here. Travel safely and let me know when you are coming."

"Okay, thanks for your help."

"Bye," he said and hung up.

Chapter 32

After she talked to Lero. Jean decided to go ahead back to Tempe. She alerted Ernie that she was coming and then drove the Grand Cherokee through the night and the desert. She kept Lero's Smith and Wesson in her purse. When she reached Ernie's building about five in the morning, she pushed the call box button at the large glass front doors. A male voice answered. "Can I help you?"

She said, "This is Jean Mathison, to see Professor Ernest Galvin."

""What's up?" asked Ernie when he arrived about seven thirty to find her in his outer office waiting room.

"We need to be ready to act. Lero and the NRO guys think they may move the package today. I came up through the desert and got her about five. The guard let me in and I took a nap on the sofa in the hall outside your office."

Jean and Ernie sat in his office/laboratory in the second sub-basement. None the graduate students were there because they were taking classes like regular students., so they had the place to themselves.

They had had breakfast in the cafeteria above and returned to work on preparations. Ernie said, "The thing I like most about the plan is that the strike equipment is Soviet or Russian. It was built by the Soviet Union and now belongs to the Russians. The beauty of it is that they don't even know about it. If we mess up on this, and the elves in Disneyland analyze the metal, they will track it back to the Ruskies. The trail that might lead to us is thin as a thread. I like the odds."

"I want to strike first with the high explosives warhead. That way, the locale will more closely resemble where an explosion took place and that the explosion set off the birthday cake. It will look like they blundered and accidentally set their own device off before it was intended to go off."

Jean asked, "But what if they excavate the site and find their device unexploded? Won't they know then that the whole thing was a foreign strike?"

"Yes, but the site will be radioactive for a while. It might be a year before they can excavate."

Jean said, "You know, since the Natanz site is so far underground, we should think about two or three strikes by high explosive warheads before the birthday cake. It is eight meters underground and covered by a ceiling that is two and a half meters of reinforced concrete. There are over a hundred thousand square feet in the complex, too. A series of explosions would not seem suspicious under the circumstances, don't you think?"

Ernie nodded, then added, "The international community is going to be furious at the elves in Disneyland. Allowing such a device to detonate above ground, like that, would be the first atmospheric detonation since nineteen eighty by the Chinese."

"My goodness, said Jean. "How much radiation and fall out will one of those devices create?"

"All this assumes that we can strike accurately before the package leave the assembly facility. Once it leaves there, we could still strike as we plan, I think. It would look like something on the road caused the device to detonate. This could make a very big mess. I would much rather have it go off underground."

Chapter 33

Lero dialed his satellite phone again. After he dialed, there was a silent pause, then an audible click, then it began to ring conventionally.

"Major Browning's office. Sergeant Myers," said the voice.

"Sergeant Myers, this is Lero. I need to speak to the Major, please."

"Sir, just now, he is offshore in a helo on a training exercise with a crew of operators. May I have him call you back?"

"Yes, of course. Do you have my number from this phone?"

"Yes, sir. I have it. Is there a better time to call?"

"Thanks, but, no, tell him to call at his earliest convenience, night or day."

"Very well, sir. Anything else?"

"No, thanks, Sergeant Myers. Good day."

"Good day, sir."

Chapter 34

Lero was working at his conference table across from his desk when the phone rang. After he said just, "Hello," the voice on the other end said, "This is Major Browning, returning your call.'

"Yes, Major Browning, this is Lero. Jefe said you could help me with some information. We are in the planning stages of a birthday party and we need some data."

"Does your party have a theme?" asked Browning.

"Yes, we are calling it 'Hoopla,'" said Lero.

"I see," said Browning. "What do you need to know, specifically."

"We need to know location and contents of safe deposit boxes in Disneyland."

(Note: In case you have not already deciphered this coded language, Lero is talking with Browning about buried weapons caches in Iran. Covert operators have, over a period of years, brought in weapons and supplies and buried them at night. Such caches are available to covert operators in country and Lero needs to find out if any contain laser designator components. Security would not permit a complete laser designator to be buried in a single cache, but the three main components of a laser designator would be buried in three separate sites.)

"I can put that together for you and fax it to you within a couple of hours. Any area that we need not include?" asked Browning.

"Yes, you may exclude the area south of about three hundred clicks south of Esfahan. Our interests concentrate elsewhere."

"Very well," said Browning. "After I send the data, let me know if you need further information. Thanks for asking us."

"Thank you, Major Browning. See you later," said Lero and hung up.

Chapter 35

When the helos approached FOB Kilo Thirteen, Sergeant Major Hopkins was waiting for them on the perforated metal pad. He stood next to a Jeep in the dark. As the helos approached, they could see his outline at the edge of the matting.

After the helos landed and settle down and the dust began to clear, he stepped forward to the nearest helo as the crewman opened the sliding hatch. The crewman put down a short ladder to let Zila climb down. Another crewman jumped down and held her hand to steady her as she climbed down.

She turned away from the helo and encountered Hopkins.

"Good evening, ma'am. Welcome to Forward Operating Base Kilo Thirteen. I am Sergeant Major Hopkins. Do you need medical attention or are you okay to ride a short distance with me?"

"Thank you so much, Sergeant. I am fine to travel. I am so grateful for the extraction. I was worried that they would be waiting for me at Mashhad."

Hopkins pointed to the jeep and they walked to it. Once on board, he drove her from the helo pad back to his office in a tent about a quarter mile away.

He escorted her into his office and offered her a seat. She sat down like someone who was weary of travel, but her face showed the excitement of freedom.

"Just wait here a moment, ma'am. I need to report that we have you with us and get directions."

"Certainly, Sergeant. I am comfortable. Take your time."

He lifted the receiver of his phone and scowled at his list of often used telephone numbers, then punched in the digits. In a few seconds, the phone connected and a voice said, "Major Browning's office."

Hopkins said, "This is Sergeant Major Hopkins at FOB Kilo Thirteen. Advise the Major that we have his package and are awaiting instructions."

"Thank you, Sergeant Major. I will forward the message immediately and one of us will call you back in a few minutes."

"Thank you. Good evening," said Hopkins and hung up.

In a few minutes the satellite phone rang. Hopkins answered, "FOB Kilo Thirteen, Sergeant Major Hopkins."

"This is Colonel Peterson, at CentCom, Sergeant Major.

"Yes sir. Good evening."

"We are very glad to get your news about the package. We will arrange for her transport after dawn. Where is the nearest runway from your location?"

"There is a four thousand foot runway at Kandahar, about fifty miles east of us, Sir, but it is a dirt runway."

"That is plenty for the aircraft we will send. Would you ask the package if she could be ready to travel later this morning from that runway? We will call back with the coordinates of the runway just to be sure your driver takes her to the correct location. Tell your men and their leadership that I am putting them in for a unit commendation for a nice piece of work."

"I will ask her about the travel, sir, but my impression is that she will be most grateful for the distance between her and trouble. Thank you very much for the unit commendation, sir. My men are first rate and give one hundred percent."

"Very good, Sergeant Major. Thanks for your efforts. Get some rest."

"Thank you, sir. Good night."

Shortly after dawn, a U.S. Army C-12 twin turboprop airplane flew downwind at the dirt strip west of Kandahar and made a nice soft field landing. . A large dust cloud enveloped the plane as it went into thrust reverse, but it had plenty of runway left when it got down to taxiing speed.

Sergeant Major Hopkins walked Zila to the aircraft and made sure she got on safely. The pilots did not even shut down the engines, but adjusted the thrust on the props to a neutral setting, so there was no prop blast. These guys are used to transporting VIPs, so they knew how to treat a lady. Hopkins wished Zila "good luck" and shut the door for her. He could see her go forward and take a seat. The C-12 did not want to waste any time on the ground, and began to move as soon as she sat down. In less than a minute, it was back on the runway with the power coming up. In a trail of blowing dust, it accelerated back down the runway and arced into a right turn to take Zila to Prince Sultan Air Base. Sergeant Major Hopkins stood for a couple of minutes to watch, and in a couple of minutes, he could not even hear the C-12. He silently wished Zila a happy life in the west.

Chapter 36

Dr. Abbasi was waiting near the door to the outside when Dr. Ferrydoon approached. The technician opened the door just in time for Dr. Ferrydoon to drive directly in without slowing down. In a moment, the door was closing behind his white Land Cruiser. Inside, he stopped and got out. When Dr. Abbasi stepped up, the two embraced like the old friends that they were.

"So glad to see you. Glad you are here safely," said Abbasi to Ferrydoon.

"Yes, praise Allah, I am safe and the package is safely here, too," he said.

Abbasi got into the Toyota with Ferrydoon and directed him as he drove them back into the mountain tunnel. He parked as Abbasi directed and they stood by as the technicians removed the container and put it on a cart to take it into the adjoining laboratory.

After the technicians finished and left, Abbasi took Ferrydoon over behind the curtain on the left side of the laboratory and showed him the device. Ferrydoon was amazed and very pleased and very grateful to be shown the culmination of thousands of hours of work and study.

The device was about eight feet long and about one and a half feet in diameter. It was contained in a brushed stainless outer cover with numerous hatches fastened by countersunk stainless screws. The beauty of the mechanism was overshadowed by the ominous aura of a horrendous weapon of mass destruction.

"Before we begin the connection, let's go get a nice meal and you can tell me about your trip," said Abbasi.

Ferrydoon nodded enthusiastically and they locked the lab and walked toward the mess hall. Ferrydoon was once again impressed with the number of people in the facility and with the cleanliness of everything. Most of the technicians wore white jump suits over their clothes and cloth boots. The mess hall was big enough to seat about two hundred at a time and there were so many people there that the arrival of Abbasi and Shahreze did not cause any stir.

"I guess I will never get over the size of this facility. How far underground are we at this position?" asked Ferrydoon.

"We are about a thousand feet back into the mountain. The distance to the surface from here is over four hundred feet," said Abbasi.

Ferrydoon merely shook his head and smiled.

As they walked back to the laboratory, Abbasi told Ferrydoon that he had reserved his old room for him, so he could stay underground with them while they were working on the connection of the trigger to the device.

"If all the connections are correctly sized, we should be able to get it connected today," he said.

They walked along toward the lab with anticipation.

Once back in the lab, with the door securely locked, they wheeled the cart with the container that Dr. Ferrydoon had brought over next to the device. Then Dr. Abbasi opened his tool chest and got out a couple of battery powered drills. He fitted each with a Phillips screwdriver bit and they began to remove the dozens of stainless countersunk screws that held the nose cone to the main body of the device. The drills made quick work, but it still took several minutes for them to remove all the screws that secured the nose cone. Dr. Abbasi showed Ferrydoon how to bring over the portable crane to lift the trigger and move it into place to be fastened to the device. It, too, was battery operated and had a large car battery in its carriage.

Once they had the nose cone off and had used the crane to gently lower it to the lab floor next to the device, they rolled the crane over next to the container with the trigger in it. They took off the cover and hooked the crane's hook to the built in loop on the side of the trigger. After gently taking up the slack in the crane's cable, they used the remote control to direct the crane to lift the trigger from its case. It weighed about a hundred fifty pounds and was roughly cylindrical and about two feet and a half long. Once hoisted clear of the container, they carefully rolled the crane with the trigger over so that the trigger was over top of the place where it would be secured to the device. Dr. Abbasi got out a box of stainless lock nuts and they prepared to connect the trigger to the device.

"Before we make the connection, perhaps it would be appropriate if we would take a break to pray about this momentous event," said Abbasi to Ferrydoon.

"Of course," said Ferrydoon and they got out their prayer blankets and put them on the floor in parallel, facing Mecca.

During their prayers, Ferrydoon was once again impressed with how quiet the lab was and there were no noises from the hallway outside, either.

Chapter 37

In a few minutes, they had gotten the trigger to the position where it could be lowered enough to line up the bolts on it with the holes in the device. As they lowered it into position, they confirmed that all the bolts lined up with their corresponding holes. When that was assured, Abbasi extended his hand to Ferrydoon to congratulate him on the correct preparation of the mounting screws. Then they juggled the trigger's bolts into the holes and spun on four nuts, one on each side and one on the top and bottom, just to hold the trigger to the device so they could snug up and properly torque each nut.

Over the next fifteen minutes, they spun on all the other nuts and methodically tightened and torqued each nut, alternating across the bolt pattern each time to tighten opposing nuts until they had them all tightened and properly torqued.

Then they took a break to admire their work and stretch their tired backs.

The next thing to do was to connect the battery and test the circuits. There were stringent protocols for the test so that the device would not become armed in the process and they double checked each other as they went through the list, item by item. They found all in order and the last few items called for a power up of the test circuit. They gave each other a significant look before Dr. Abasssi pushed the correct buttons to call for a circuit test from the device. They both tensed up, but sure enough, the LED lights came on in the correct sequence and pattern to indicate that, indeed, the device was operational.

After a relieved sigh from them both, Dr. Abbasi powered down the system and they went over to his desk to rest and reflect.

He got a bottle of fruit juice from his refrigerator and they sat in silence for a few moments, each pouring out a healthy swig from the bottle into his paper cup.

Finally, Dr. Shahreze spoke: "Praise Allah. It appears to be working properly. I have instructions from the most high that we should not attempt to report this, but to carry on and go forward with the test."

"That is my understanding, also," said Abbasi. "Let's walk down to the motor pool and pick a truck for the transport."

"A pleasure," said Ferrydoon. They went out, locked the door carefully, threw the empty fruit juice cartons in the trash bucket outside the door of the lab and walked farther into the tunnel.

As it came time for the truck to leave to take the assembled device to the test site, Dr. Abassi said to Ferrydoon, "I want you to go to the test with us. You deserve that after all the work you and your people did to design and fabricate the trigger. However, due to security precautions, you will either have to sit and the back of the truck or wear sand blasted goggles so you cannot see details if you want to sit up front with me and the driver. The trip is several hours, so we will take food and drink so we will not have to stop where we might be seen. We will stop to eliminate along the way when we are sure we are not being observed. Which do you prefer?"

"I will sit up front with you and the driver. Even if I cannot see details, I will be able to converse with you along the way," said Ferrydoon.

"Very well. We will dress and pack and visit the facilities here. We will leave as soon as it is dark. There will be time to take a short nap, if you want."

"A good plan. Thank you," said Ferrydoon.

Chapter 38

The AWACS currently on station over the western half of Afghanistan was loitering at forty thousand feet, westbound, about fifty miles inside the border with Iran.

Sergeant Melody Branch keyed her mike and spoke to the duty officer, Captain Murphy.

"Captain, we have activity at the site you wanted me to watch."

"I will be right back," he said as he got up quickly from his seat and started back down the aisle.

"What do you have?" he asked as he swung a folding chair up behind her at her console.

"Consistent with orders, I gave this truck the number eleven when it exited just five minutes ago. It is the first truck to come out since the order was given. From its appearance, it is a double rear axle two and a half ton military truck. The bed is covered with a fitted tarp. I noted the time of exit as nineteen thirty four, local. You can see it here on the screen." She gestured to show him which object she was talking about.

"Our station will take us about forty miles west, then turn around and fly east about a hundred miles. Do you think you can stay in visual contact with the truck while we continue west?" he asked.

"Yes, sir. The only challenge is our link to the satellite and it is just fine right now, with a full strength signal. We are good to continue west."

"Good work, Sergeant. Advise if the truck stops and keep track of the routes on the ground that it takes until further notice," he said.

"Will do, sir," she said and turned her attention again totally to the screen.

Captain Murphy returned to his station near the front of the cabin. He immediately dialed his communication radio to a discrete frequency and called, "Jupiter, this is Calisto."

A short pause accompanied by the crackle of mild static filled his headset, then, "Calisto, this is Jupiter. Go ahead."

"Jupiter, we have a good prospect in sight. We are monitoring its progress, but wanted to report as soon as we could."

"Good. Maintain contact. Report any stops, report at least once every twenty minutes."

"Will do," said Murphy.

"Jupiter out," said the voice.

Next the duty officer dialed a number on his satellite phone. After two rings a female voice answered, "Qatari Productions," she said.

"This is Major Taylor at NRO. Tell Lero we are monitoring a good prospect. Have him call me at this number."

"Will do, sir. Thanks for the heads up."

Lero's satellite phone buzzed. He was sitting next to it studying a chart of the central desert of Iran. He was so lost in concentration that he jumped when it rang. He recovered quickly and grabbed the phone, pressing the send button as he grasped it.

"Hello," he said.

"This is Qatari Productions, Jupiter advises they have a good prospect in sight and are monitoring its progress, now thirty clicks east of Site E."

"Thank you, Qatari. Please keep me advised."

"Will do, sir. Good evening."

Lero dialed the satellite phone, a number he knew by heart.

"Hello," said Jean.

"Say the word," he said.

"Durango," she said. What is the good word?"

"Houston," he said.

"What is your twenty?" she asked.

"Military Forty Six," he said. "Our watchbirds have a good prospect. Left the nest about thirty three minutes ago, eastbound. Military truck. They are monitoring. It is now about thirty clicks east of Site E. I don't think we can try anything while it is in motion. We just need to follow this prospect and any other good prospects until they reach their destinations and then plan something. What is your twenty?"

"I am at Site Fifteen, camping out, and standing by. Our friend and I are taking eight hour shifts, overlapping by four, so we can get some sleep. How are you?"

"I am fine. The trip in the fast bird was amazing. The trip over was only about eight hours. One aerial refueling off the east coast. The guys let me ride in the jump seat when I wanted to. Great ride."

"When this is over, can we take a trip or something? We are way behind on some things."

"Of course. Right now, I don't want to let myself be distracted by such a pleasant thought, though. Maybe we could go to Big Sur again."

"That would be so nice. Our friend advises that we need thirty five minutes to make something happen on our end."

"Thanks. I will put that into the planning. Take care. See you soon."

"You take care too. Bye."

The phone disconnected.

Next, Lero keyed in a familiar number on his satellite phone.

"Hello," said the female voice.

"This is Lero. May I speak to Mr. Murfree?"

"Sir, he and the First Lady returned from an outdoor reception on the east lawn just a few minutes ago. It was very hot and they wanted to change before resuming duties. I expect him back in twenty minutes or so. Shall I put your call through to the residence?"

"No, don't disturb them. Just tell him for me that we have a prospect about thirty clicks east of Site E and ask him to call me at his convenience. We are watching it closely. I don't think anything is going to happen for a while."

"Very well, sir. Thank you."

He hung up.

Chapter 39

The phone on Ernie's desk rang. He answered after the first ring.

"Hello."

"Hold a moment for Mr. Murfree," said the female voice.

"This is Mr Murfree. Say the word."

Ernie spoke the word "Trinity" into the telephone.

"Now, we have just two problems," said the President. "We have to tail that truck to wherever they are taking the device for the test, and then we have to get a team in there near enough to paint the target. How long after they arrive at the test site do you think they will conduct the test?"

Ernie paused a minute while he thought. "Sir, I would think that they will first want to rest a bit after a long bumpy trip in a military truck. Then they will want to make sure the site is prepared. Then they will want to run systems checks on the device and any monitoring equipment they have installed. Then they will set the timing for the detonation and move out to watch from a distance. All that is going to take a day, at least."

"Thanks," Ernie. "I will keep you in touch."

"My pleasure, sir. Good day."

Chapter 40

"I know it is a long shot and a bit weird, but I have an idea how to get a man into laser range of the test site," said Lero.

"I am all ears," said General McRay. "What is your idea?"

"Why don't we fit up a composite sail plane. A composite sailplane would not show up on anybody's radar and we could use the altitude to make sure we reached the site area. Use fiberglass oxygen bottles and offload any metal objects in the aircraft, like radios. Tow the sailplane to about thirty thousand feet over western Afghanistan and have the pilot fly near to the test site, land, incinerate the sailplane, hide and light up the site for the party. One man in and only one man to exfiltrate."

"That just might work," said McRay. "How soon could you get a sailplane upfitted and get it to Shindand or Bagram?"

"I have a friend who can have a crated Sparrowhawk ready to ship later today. It is in Hawaii and I am going to need transport to Shindand Air Base. Perhaps we could get a B-1 on a training mission to fly it to Bagram. I could hitch a ride to Bagram and get it over to Shindad by helo. I can use one of their hangars to upfit it there. Deciding on a tow plane that was slow enough but could get us up to thirty thousand will require some study. I will get back to you on that."

"Okay, have your supplier have a crated Sparrowhawk ready to load. I will call my people and have them arrange rapid transit as soon as possible. Our guys will pick it up and fly it to Bagram."

"Where will you get a pilot in time?" asked McRay.

"There is not time to look around. I will have to fly it," said Lero. "I have six hundred hours in sailplanes and we are in a hurry."

There was a considerable silence as General McRay digested the whole suggested idea.

"Okay. Let's do it."

"Thanks, General. I will get going to Bagram. Thanks."

"You are welcome. Good luck. Be careful."

They hung up.

Chapter 41

Lero looked up a number in his phone book. He dialed"

"Air Ops, CentCom, Major McReady," came the answer on the second ring.

"Major McReady, this is Lero, working on the Hoopla Project. I need an L-6 Laser Designator and transport for myself and baggage from Prince Sultan to Bagram, your earliest availability."

"Roger, Lero. Let me check and I will call you back."

"Thanks, Major, Good evening."

Lero looked at his watch. It was seven PM local time. The airbase was not nearly as active at this hour as it was in the early morning, but it was still pretty busy. He began to throw items of equipment and clothing into his duffel.

Ten minutes into his scrambled packing effort, the phone rang.

"Lero, this is McReady. Your transport is taxiing out to leave Diego Garcia., estimating Prince Sultan in an hour and twenty minutes. Coordinate with local air traffic control to agree on a place to meet it and board. Your laser designator will be waiting for you at Shindand Air Base. Good luck."

"Thanks, Major McReady. Appreciate the quick work."

"You are welcome. I don't know any details about what you are into, but good luck. Let us know if we can help."

"Okay, good evening."

They hung up. By now, Lero was wearing military fatigues and flight boots and was checking to see if he had his prescription dark glasses and his hand held transceiver. Once he was sure of his packing job and reviewed what was packed, he called the Motor Pool.

"Motor pool, Sergeant Faraday," came the answer.

"This is Mr. Roman at the contractor's quarters. Could you have someone pick me up and take me to the flight line?"

"Yes, sir. A driver will pick you up at your front door in ten minutes. Dark blue Ford LTD."

"Thanks, Sergeant Faraday. Good evening."

They hung up.

Chapter 42

Lero lugged his heavy duffel over to the door. He turned to look back at the quarters he had used for the last four days and thought to himself that he probably would never see it again. It was not the only place he had had to leave like this over the years, but each was a moment he liked to remember. He satisfied himself, turned off the light and lugged the duffel into the hall. He closed and locked the door and picked up the duffel again. At the front desk, he put the key down on the shelf on the top of the lower half of the divided door and spoke to the desk sergeant through the open top of the doorway.

"Leaving your quarters, Sergeant. Thanks for the hospitality."

"You are welcome, Sir. Good luck and come back to see us."

"Thanks again," said Lero and went out the front door with his duffel.

The sweltering heat of Saudi Arabia hit him in the face like a slap. He was very thankful that the blue Ford arrived as promised. The driver popped the trunk and Lero muscled his duffel inside and climbed in the passenger seat. The interior was air conditioned and gave some respite from the heat. The trip to the flight line took only a couple of minutes, but it would have exhausted him to have lugged the duffel over there in that heat. The sun was setting as he got out at the flight line parking lot.

There was an airman waiting for him in the operations center. As soon as he stepped in with his duffel, the airman approached.

"Mr. Roman, are you ready to go?"

"Yes," said Lero and the airman swung the duffel and pointed to the aircraft waiting on the tarmac. The ominous and powerful silhouette of a B-1 was between Lero and the remnants of the sunset. He and the airman walked quickly to the ladder that another airman was holding. The airman carrying Lero's duffel reached it up to a waiting hand extending from the belly hatch. Lero stopped long enough to shake the hand of the airman who had greeted him and hustled up the ladder. He could hear the number one engine begin to spool up as he climbed. By the time the crewmember got him to his seat, all four engines were running and the brakes released with a slight jar.

Lero knew that the pilots would have their hands full and that they knew where they were to take him, so he let them do their jobs and tried to relax. What lay ahead of him was daunting and fraught with risk, but in the lurch, there was no one else qualified to do what had to be done and it had to be done as fast as possible. The test might even beat him to the punch. He hoped the Overhead guys were tracking the correct vehicle and that he could be ready and in position before they set off the test.

When the B-1 pilots applied full throttle for takeoff, Lero was pressed firmly back in his seat. It was a good minute before he felt it let up any. Out the small window by his seat, he could see the last vestiges of the sunset and a black sky above it. By now, they were over the Persian Gulf going east to avoid Iranian airspace. They would turn north after they reached Pakistan. He tried to relax and doze, but he could not. His mind was whirling with ideas and plans.

It surprised him how soon they changed course toward the north. It could not have been forty minutes since they took off from Prince Sultan. It gave a whole new meaning to "rapid transit." He smiled and was grateful this speedy bomber was "ours."

In another thirty minutes, he could feel the great plane slow and he could feel the wings extend from the swept back position to almost straight out for slower flight. The bomber only made one turn on its approach to Bagram and touched down smoothly. When the brakes had cooled enough, they taxied to the ramp and shut down. The pilots came back from the flight deck and shook hands with him. He thanked them for the hop and went with them out the hatch in the belly.

Chapter 43

A U. S. Army Sergeant was waiting for him when they handed down his duffel. Lero lowered it to the tarmac as the Sergeant stepped up.

"Sir, Sergeant Pickering. Let me take that for you. The vehicle is the black Ford sedan over there" and he pointed to it. They walked quickly to the Ford and the Sergeant heaved the duffel gently into the trunk and they got in. Once they were in the car, the Sergeant said, "Your package from Hawaii is scheduled to arrive in about half an hour. They have arranged for an CH47 to take you and it to Shindand as soon as they can load it. If you want to grab a quick dinner, I can take you to the mess hall."

"That would be great, but first I need to visit the latrine," said Lero.

"There is one at the mess hall. We will be there in less than a minute."

"As I get older, my bladder seems to get smaller, Sergeant Pickering."

"Understood, sir. You don't have many more years on your meter than I do and I already notice that, too."

His dinner was a nice beef stew like you would expect stateside, with dark gravy and mashed potatoes and a nice Jello salad and iced tea. Sergeant Pickering let Lero eat in peace and waited for him on a bench near the front door of the mess hall. It was between meals for Pickering or he would have joined Lero at mess.

As Pickering saw Lero push his chair back, he got up from his seat and was waiting for Lero at the door. They got back into the Ford and Pickering drove them to a hangar across the base. It took four minutes or so. Lero was impressed with how dark and how quiet the base was. The hangar was much larger than the CH47 required, but it was secure. Sergeant Pickering gave the sentry a code word and he opened the door for them. . The crate from Hawaii was being loaded as they stepped in.

"This is where I leave you, sir. Do you need anything else?"

"No, thanks, Sergeant Pickering. Good luck to you. Thanks again."

They shook hands and Pickering turned to leave.

Chapter 44

Lero strode over to the crew loading the crate. It was twenty feet long and about four feet square on the end. The ground crew chief stepped up and saluted.

"Sir, we will have you ready to go in just a few minutes. Do you need anything else from us before you go?"

"No, Sergeant. Nice work. I appreciate your help. I will take it from here."

"Very good, sir. I will get someone to load your duffel. You can board through the door on the left front of the fuselage."

As Lero settled into the seat, the tug gave the helo a little jolt and began to tow it out onto the tarmac. The big doors of the hangar opened to let them out. Once outside, they towed the CH47 out about a hundred yards from the hangar and stopped. When the tug operator disconnected his tow bar, he gave a hand signal to the pilots and the big rotors began to slowly turn. Lero imagined that the pilots were calling for clearance to depart. In a couple of minutes, the helo began to move forward and it rolled only about ten feet before it lifted off into the night. Lero had forgotten how noisy a CH47 can be, especially in military trim. He reached for the ear plugs in the pocket on the bulkhead next to his seat and put them in his ears quickly. The helo did not seem to turn at all, but simply climbed into the night. On this flight he was tired enough to sleep a little. In about half an hour, the change in pitch of the rotors awakened him and he was fully awake when the CH47 touched down. The pilots shut down the rotors and another tug backed into position to hook on. All the crew stayed in position while the tug towed the CH47 into a hangar. Once inside, they turned on enough lights so one could see, not bright, but sufficient.

An officer stepped up. "Major Hallibrand, sir. Welcome to Shindand Air Base. Did you have a pleasant flight?"

"It was nice and smooth. Thank you."

"CentCom said this was a special operation. I have made two mechanics with security clearances available and they are ready to start as soon as you are. I will leave you to your work. If you need anything from me, have one of them call. I will be available through the night."

"Thanks, Major. I will call if we need anything."

"The crew will have the crate out and the helo out of your way shortly. If you need to visit the latrine, it is to the right there, across the hangar. I will leave you to your work. Good luck."

Chapter 45

As soon as he was alone, Lero got out his satellite phone and dialed a familiar number. After two rings a female voice answered, "Hello."

"This is Lero to speak to Mr. Murfree."

"Just a moment, please," she said. Lero looked at his watch and did the math. The time in D.C. would be about seven P.M.

"This is Mr. Murfree," said the familiar voice.

"This is Lero, good evening."

"Say the word, please."

"Houston."

"What's up?" asked the President.

'I am at Shindand Air Base. I have a Duckhawk sailplane in a crate, in a secure hangar, and two technicians with security clearances to help me assemble it. What is the temperature in Disneyland?"

"The Overhead guys can give Jean and Ernie the coordinates of the party. The lastest report is that the chicken made it across the road and is on the nest. We think the gestation period is eight hours or less from now."

"Do you still want us to crash the party, sir?" asked Lero.

"Before I give the OK, I would like to have your plan in mind," said the President.

"Sir, with you approval, I will assemble this sailplane, get my gear ready, including the magic marker they sent, whistle up a tow to about flight level three zero zero, then aviate to the vicinity of the party, land, torch the bird, find a good point of observation and inform Jean and Ernie. The plan is to start with a firecracker before the light show. If the overhead people are confident of the address, Ernie says we can arrive within a quarter mile based on the technology in place, but using the magic marker, we can find a location within a few feet. He says deflection is very limited at those speeds, though, so the address has to be pretty accurate."

"How confident are you guys that we can get the thing close enough to the correct address?" asked the President.

"Ernie says we can be confident of less than thirty feet with the magic marker, sir," said Lero.

"Very well, you have my authority to proceed as you propose. Take care of yourself. I will be praying for you. Come back to us in one piece, please," said the President.

"Very well, sir. Thank you for your confidence in us. Good evening."

The President crossed the dining room of the residence and sat down with Janice.

"Is everything alright?" she asked.

"There is going to be a nasty accident, I am afraid," he said.

"I know you have thought a lot about it. I am confident you have done the right thing, dear," she said.

"Is there time to pray about it?" she asked.

"Yes, we have time to pray," he said solemnly.

"Is one of our friends involved?" she asked.

"Yes," said the President as he scooped some steamed peas onto his plate.

Chapter 46

Next, Lero dialed Jean's number.

"Hello," she said.

"Hello, say the word, please."

"Sedona. What is your word?"

"Houston."

There was a short pause.

"Where are you. We have been worried."

"I am at Shindand Air Base in western Afghanistan."

"What is going on?" she asked.

"The party is on. I got directions from management. We are to proceed. Noisemaker first, followed by the big enchilada, if necessary. I will use a Duckhawk sailplane to get into position. They have a magic marker for me and all the gear I need. We are putting the wings on right now. I will probably be on my way in a couple of hours. I will advise by sat phone and then we can communicate by radio once I am aloft."

"How in the world are you going to do it in that kind of aircraft?" she asked.

I will get a tow from an MQ-9 up to three zero zero near the border. I will aviate to the party, land, incinerate the plane, then find a good place to watch the show."

"Oh, my goodness. If you are close enough to do all that, won't you be in danger?" she asked.

"There will be enhanced risk, I think, but this needs to be done and I am the only one to do it. Security is tight. If anything goes wrong, remember these were the best two years of my life."

There was a long pause.

With her voice quivering, she said, "Oh, my, Dan. Be careful. Come back to me."

"I will be careful. The overhead guys will supply you with the address. Be ready for my call and we can make this happen."

"Can you give me an idea where we are to make things happen?"

"About four hundred clicks west of present position. Worked out salt mine. Remote. I will have our guys transmit the lat and long to Ernie, so you guys can calibrate from your end."

"Alright, then. Go do your thing. Remember how dear you are to me and try to be safe."

"You are as dear to me, too. I will be careful. I love you, Jean."

"I love you, too. Call me when you are airborne on the usual frequency."

"Will do. Bye."

"Bye."

Chapter 47

Lero consulted the telephone number chart on the wall of the hangar. He used the local telephone to dial.

"Quartermaster, Sergeant Teague speaking."

"Sergeant Teague, this is Lero in Hangar 8. I have a list of requested items when you are ready to copy."

"Right, sir, we were alerted that you would call. What do you need?"

"I need a square canopy black parachute, lightest weight you have, a satellite telephone with an anonymous number, a hand held radio for aviation frequencies, a flight helmet, size seven and a quarter, with an oxygen mask, two "N" bottles of oxygen and a regulator, a pair of sunglasses, a Demron Radiation suit, a couple of those astronaut aluminum blankets, three days of MREs, a dozen bottles of Gatorade 2, an EPIRB if you have one, a pocket GPS, a non-government issue side arm with an extra magazine, fifty rounds of ammunition, a powerful flashlight with an infrared filter, a light weight radar reflector, a pair of long range binoculars, a pair of night vision goggles, a one hundred foot skein of black nylon rope, a Swiss Army knife, a boarding party issue knife, a rucksack and a pharmaceutical kit."

Sergeant Teague read the list back to Lero.

Lero said, "That is it, thanks."

"We have those items here on the base. It will take a little while to round them up and get them to you. Is two hours alright?" asked Teague.

"That would be just fine, Sergeant Teague. The person who delivers it needs to have a security clearance."

"What is the password for the sentry, sir."

"Tripwire," said Lero.

"Got it, sir. See you in a couple hours."

"Thanks,Sergeant Teague. Good evening."

Chapter 48

Tech Sergeants Rice and Amburgey already had the end off of the crate when Lero joined them near the center of the hangar. Together, they slid the wings and fuselage out of the crate on the blankets they had laid out. The horizontal stabilizer was fastened to the crate on the open end. They put all the components out in the orientation that they would be fastened together and opened the box of fasteners. Rice took the instruction booklet and read to them as they began to assemble the all composite Duckhawk.

"I was just thinking, sir," said Amburgey, "Aren't you hungry and thirsty after the trip?"

"I was so focused, I guess I forgot," said Lero. "Can we get some sandwiches and drinks sent up?"

"Sure," said Amburgey. "I will order some."

He went to the phone on the wall.

"It says that the first items are the wings. They fit into the slot in the sides of the fuselage and there are pins that pass through the spars to hold them in place. Five pins, in the bag marked "1." The left wing spar goes in front of the right wing spar and they get pinned to the bulkhead using the trap door in the top of the fuselage. "What is the empty weight of this plane, sir?" asked Amburgey. "It looks pretty light."

"The empty weight is one hundred ninety nine pounds," said Lero.

"Wow," said Amburgey.

Lero used his satellite phone to make another call.

"CentCom ops center, Major Vorholt, speaking.

"Major, this is Lero. I am at Foxtrot Fifteen. Can you make an MQ-9 available to me in about three hours? I will need a lift upstairs. It will be towing a sailplane up to flight level three zero zero over at the Iranian border, then release me and return to you. The code word for the mission is Hoopla. Do you need any further information?"

"No, sir, that will be fine. I have your number, sir. I will call you back with an availability. Good evening."

"Thanks, Major." Lero hung up.

(Note to the technically inclined: An MQ-9 is a drone. Nicknamed the Reaper, it is powered by a nine hundred fifty horsepower turboprop engine, weighs eleven thousand seven hundred pounds fully fueled, can carry a substantial load of bombs or missiles, has an eighty eight foot wing span and can stay aloft for forty two hours. This is the big brother of the Predator drone.)

Just as they were positioning the horizontal stabilizer on the empennage, the satellite phone rang. Lero asked with his eyes if he could let them hold position while he answered. They nodded. He went quickly to his phone in the chair by the chart table.

"Hello."

"This is Vorholt. An MQ-9 will arrive at Foxtrot Fifteen in approximately two hours. Say position you want it to come to."

"Fifty yards south of Hangar 8."

"Got it. We will alert air traffic control. Good luck."

"Thanks, Major and thank everyone who helped you make this possible."

"You are welcome. Just be careful. Good luck." He rang off.

Chapter 49

As Lero put the satellite phone back in the chair. The sentry knocked on the door and came in with a package. He put it down quickly and went back out to his duty station.

Amburgey went over and retrieved the food package. They took a break and ate the sandwiches and fruit and cookies and drank bottles of Gatorade 2.

The sailplane was almost assembled. The control cables, made of carbon fiber would be the next thing. They would not show up on radar at all. The cables protruded from the wing roots and the empennage and only had to be connected to the bell cranks. They were already adjusted and only needed a pin and keeper to be connected to the pilot's controls. In a little more than an hour, they had the sailplane assembled.

"Would you happen to have any green or gray paint in spray cans?" asked Lero.

"Sure, what would an Army base be without green paint?" asked Rice.

"Lets just spray some on the sailplane, to break up the color a bit. That bright white needs some softening. I don't think I will be flying much in daylight, but a little camo would help."

"Sure," said Rice and went over to get a case of spray cans.

Now things were coming together.

The sentry knocked on the door again and motioned them over.

"Sir, the Quartermaster is here with the gear you ordered. He wants you to sign for it. How should I handle this?"

"We will turn off the lights. One of you drive the truck in here alone.   We will return his truck as soon as we have unloaded it. Have him wait outside. And tell him thanks for his quick work."

"Will do, Sir," said the sentry and went out the door.

Rice went over and turned off the lights in the interior, then opened the doors.

The pickup truck came in with the sentry driving and halted just inside the doors.

Amburgey closed the doors and he and Rice met Lero at the tailgate to unload all the material. They laid out all the items on the hangar floor next to the sailplane and Lero double checked to see if all items were there. Once they were certain, Lero signed the paper on the clip board and gave it to Rice to give to the sentry who would pass it on to the quartermaster. Rice drove the pickup back out of the hangar doors and Amburgey shut them again.

Lero tried on the helmet and it fit nicely. Then he slung on the parachute and adjusted the straps for the correct length. Then he took off the helmet and the parachute harness.

"I guess it is going to be a little cramped in the cockpit, but I think everything will fit. Let's get as much into the space behind the seat as we can. A rearward center of gravity will enhance glide range. Let's put only those items I will need in flight in front of the seat near my feet.

With the three of them working, it did not take long to get everything into the cockpit. The canopy would close over it all, so Lero was pleased.

Once we depart, I will need the hand held transceiver and the two GPS units, my charts, and a bottle of Gatorade up front. The oxygen bottles look fine behind the seat. Nice job plumbing them together, fellows."

"Will you be aloft for a long time, sir?" asked Rice.

"We figure about two and a half hours," said Lero.

"Would you want to take a relief bottle, sir?" asked Amburgey.

"Good idea. Just put it where I can see it from the seat," said Lero.

The telephone on the east wall rang. Amburgey was the closest. He took a message and returned to the sailplane.

"Sir, air traffic control says the MQ-9 will taxi up and stop in the next five minutes. Should be something to watch."

Lero nodded and the three of them went over to the personnel door next to the big double doors to watch. The door was blacked out except for a small slit about an inch tall and eighteen inches wide. As they crowded to watch, the ominous shape of the MQ-9 materialized out of the light fog. As they had asked, it taxied up to the hangar and turned to be facing away from the hangar and shut down. In its gray paint and without any markings of any kind, it was an eerie sight sitting on the tarmac in remote Afghanistan.

Lero and the airmen returned to the sailplane. They double checked all the control surfaces and their actions within the arcs of movement designed into them.

Chapter 50

Lero went over to the west wall and dialed his satellite phone.

"Hello," Jean said.

"Hi. It's me. I am ready to go from Hangar Eight at Foxtrot Fifteen. You and Ernie are in control now. I have briefed the drone controllers in the cab at Bagram, but you will need to call them now and tell them that we are ready to go in five minutes. If you lose voice contact with me for more than half an hour, scrub the mission and report to Mr. Murfree. When I get in position, I will call on the satellite phone, using the directional antenna. I know it's kinda corny, but thanks for everything. I could not do this without you."

"This is the hardest thing you have ever asked me to do. I just hope and pray that it all goes well. Please be careful and be safe. I love you."

"I love you, too. Bye."

"Bye."

He walked out of the hangar with Rice and Amburgey. The drone sat a little more than fifty yards away. It was amazing to realize that the men controlling it sat in a trailer at Bagram Air Base about two hundred miles away and that the mission would be soon taken over by the guys at Creech Air Base in Nevada, almost eight thousand miles away, and that Jean and Ernie would be in charge of the mission from here on from his laboratory in the second sub-basement in Tempe, Arizona..

They connected the tow cable to the hook in the bottom of the vertical stabilizer under the tail of the drone and walked it back to where they would connect the sailplane. Then they went into the hangar and rolled the sailplane out. The plan was to have the drone tow the sailplane out to the runway using only about fifty feet of tow rope, but when they were on the runway, Lero would extend the tow rope to fifty yards for the tow aloft. Once aloft, Lero was the sole controller of the tow rope. He would release it when they got to the altitude and location he wanted.

Lero got into the seat and Rice brought the canopy over until it only lacked about six inches from closing. They waited for the call from Creech. In about forty seconds, the phone rang.

Lero answered.

"Yes, sir. We are good to go. Once you taxi out to Runway Seventeen left, I will extend the tow rope to fifty yards."

There was a brief pause. Then the voice on the phone said, "Drone start will take place in one minute. Clear the area."

Lero spoke to Rice and Amburgey. "Thanks, fellows. I know you cannot talk about your work here tonight, but we all appreciate your help. Take care. Thanks."

He shook hands with them both and Amburgey closed the canopy.

Chapter 51

In less than ten seconds after that, the MQ-9's propeller began to turn.

Lero looked at his watch. It was one thirty, local time. Just as he determined that, the tow rope came taut and jerked the little sail plane forward. Usually, the sailplane was accelerated from standing still to enough speed for the wings to level the aircraft quickly, but tonight, the right wing dragged its tiny roller on the pavement as they taxied out the remaining three hundred yards to the south threshold of Runway Eighteen. When they reached the runway, the drone did not hesitate at the hold line, but went directly onto the runway. It achieved the center line and after a slight pause, it began to accelerate. In just a few seconds, Lero and the sailplane were on the main wheel and a few seconds after that, it lifted off, even though the drone was still on the runway. He allowed the sailplane to lift above the prop wash of the drone and waited for it to break ground. In another eight or so seconds, the drone lifted off the runway and accelerated straight ahead. As they passed over the north end of the runway, the drone began a smooth slow turn to the left, or west. Lero had adjusted the altimeter on the runway and it now read nine thousand two hundred feet. The sensitive rate of climb indicator showed they were climbing at eight hundred feet a minute. This would be a challenging flight once released even if it were in good visibility, because, at night, over remote western Afghanistan and eastern Iran, there would be very few, if any lights on the ground. It would be almost as difficult as an instrument flight.

He checked the altimeter again. Fourteen thousand six hundred. His directional gyro indicated a heading of two seven three. He had asked them to install an electric gyro for this flight in case he flew into instrument conditions because at the altitudes he intended to fly, any moisture would freeze and a vacuum instrument might become useless. The battery on board was capable of powering all the systems on board for six hours. There was no generator or alternator to recharge the battery. This was a one way flight.

As they climbed into the moonlit night, Lero could see the terrain continue to flatten the farther west they went. He got out his flashlight, held it in his mouth and pulled up his chart so he could look at it. The test site was marked with a small black circle. The distance between Shindand and the circle was about three hundred fifty miles, but he would ride behind the Reaper to very near the border between Afghanistan and Iran. The hook release lever, a large red handle on the left side of the cockpit would be pulled when he wanted to be released. His GPS showed that he was now about two hundred miles from the test site. He waited for the signal from the guys at Overhead that it was time to release. The altimeter read twenty seven thousand feet. He had started oxygen flow when they climbed through ten thousand feet. There was plenty of oxygen for this hop. The tank would feed him at this rate for six hours, if necessary. The GPS had a program to tell him what the winds were aloft and he made note of it. Forty knots from zero eight zero, a quartering tail wind. Good. That would shorten the trip.

It felt weird not being able to converse with the pilot of the airplane towing him aloft. The Reaper pulled them energetically into the night. The altimeter showed thirty thousand two hundred as the Reaper leveled off. When they stabilized, the airspeed read one hundred thirty knots, approximately one hundred fifty miles per hour, indicated air speed. This is the airspeed the wing thinks it is flying. True airspeed at this altitude would be substantially greater than indicated airspeed. The latitude and longitude readouts rolled over steadily. The outside temperature was minus thirteen Celcius, normal for this altitude. It was a nice smooth night. The stars and moon gave a nice canopy for his flight. He allowed himself a moment to think of Jean. She and Ernie were in the laboratory in Tempe, no doubt, glued to their instruments and listening carefully for communications.

Chapter 52

His elapsed time on the clock on the instrument panel indicated that it had been thirty seven minutes since they taxied onto the runway at Shindand. He took a swig of Gatorade and put the bottle back in the slot to the right of his seat.

The earphones in his helmet crackled. It was the first sound he had heard since takeoff.

Then a voice said, "Parting is such sweet sorrow," a line from Romeo and Juliet, but also his signal to release. He did a quick check of things and reached for the red handle. There was a slight jar and a mechanical noise as the little Duckhawk parted company with the Reaper. He immediately pulled the control yoke back a little, to slow his aircraft relative to the Reaper and to get a little more altitude. He watched as the Reaper slipped away into the blackness below. Now, he was completely on his own. Using his GPS, he could see that the distance to the test site was one hundred eighty miles. At the normal glide speed of one hundred twenty five miles per hour, it would take approximately an hour and a half. But, taking the tailwind into consideration, it would be shorter by about fifteen minutes. He watched the vertical speed indicator as it hovered between one hundred and one hundred fifty feet per minute. Good rate. Now, his task was to steer the correct course, considering the wind, to get him close to the test site. He tried an initial heading of two eight zero to see if that would keep him on the course line on the GPS. In five minutes, he realized that he needed to turn a couple of degrees to the right to get the plane to hold the line to the test site. Now, he was on two eight three degrees and the airspeed continued to hover about one hundred twenty five miles per hour. It had been twenty minutes since separation. He had lost only two hundred feet of altitude. So far, so good.

(Note to the technically inclined: Airspeed references in the text are for true airspeed. The airspeed indicator is adjusted from indicated air speed to true airspeed by adjusting it for the altitude at which the aircraft is flying. True to his craft, Lero has made the adjustment and is reading and flying true airspeed.)

The terrain below was hillier now, but not a problem. He would overfly these hills and land in the central desert where the terrain was much smoother. He glided on in the darkness. A sailplane is quite quiet, especially compared to a powered airplane of similar size. He marveled at how silently he slipped through the night. He knew that the guys in the cab on the airport at Bagram, and at Creech Air Base in Nevada, and Jean and Ernie knew where he would be on the flight plan, but without a transponder, the plane was invisible to any electronic observation. They would have a pip on their screen to tell them where he should be, but that was only what was planned.

He thought about Antoine de St. Exupery's book "Night Flight" as he looked up at the stars. He said a prayer for Tony who disappeared on a photo recon mission in World War II in an F-5, a converted P-38. He was never found.

Chapter 53

In the laboratory at Tempe, Jean and Ernie watched as the simulator showed a small white dot where Lero and the Duckhawk were supposed to be, based on the flight plan and the latest report. It crept toward the west over the map of Iran. They knew that a small composite sail plane like the Duckhawk would be invisible to radar, but there was still the nagging worry because of the importance of the mission and the heightened security they thought would be in place because of the test. Still, the little white dot continued to crawl across the map.

"We had better get ourselves ready," said Ernie. Do you want to man the keyboard, or read instructions from the manual we have created? With the two of us, we won't need to involve any of my grad students in this and we can keep it close to the vest.

"Why don't you read, since you created the manual? I can type instructions as you direct and you can watch over me to make sure I do it right," said Jean.

"Good idea. I will get another chair," said Ernie.

When he came back over with the chair, he scooted a small table over next to Jean's station at the computer. Then he went to the map of the college campus on the wall. Jean wondered why he would be consulting that map, since he knew the campus like the back of his hand.

Her answer came as he swung the chart away from the wall to reveal the door of a safe, built into the wall. He turned the dial first one way, then the other, four different directions. Then he turned the handle and opened the door. Inside were numerous books and portfolios. He chose one with a blue cover and put it down on the table. Then he closed the safe door and swung the campus map back into place.

The blue notebook was about four inches thick. It was a three ring binder. The cover was well worn and the corners were frayed. The cover had the deceptive title written on it: "Anaylsis of Radiotelescope data from the Green Bank Array." Ernie brought the notebook over next to Jean and put it on the table. He put on his glasses as he sat down.

"Even though this is the culmination of years of work, it is still pretty frightening to think of the power we are about to unleash."

"Well, if it is any comfort, the decision to use Module Eighteen was made by the most powerful people in our country. We are only their right arm. Still it is an eerie feeling, communicating with a satellite for the first time after it has been in orbit for thirty five years. I sure hope it wakes up for us," said Jean. "What is the first instruction?"

"First, we need to be sure that our transmitter is on the correct frequency. With digital controls it is much easier than the analog dials we used to have. The correct frequency is thirteen decimal eight five five five gigahertz.. It is about the middle of the K underband. Go ahead and get that frequency set."

Jean turned a dial on her console until the screen display of the transmitter read 13.8555 GhZ.

"Okay," she said, "Frequency set."

"Next set the power of the transmitter at thirty kilowatts."

Jean twisted another dial and brought the power up to thirty kilowatts.

"This is a big moment for me. I have worked on Module Eighteen, off and on, for over twenty five years," he said. "Voices from the past keep coming back to me. I remember what President Reagan said to me when he gave me this assignment."

"Ernie, we know you are the best person to do this for us. We are confident in you. If we can decipher the codes, this can be a very valuable asset for the United States. Call me whenever you need to. I won't interfere with your work, but just know that we will be praying for you and for our country."

"It is like he is here with us now. His expression showed me that he really believed in me and our country. He was such a great man. I will never forget it."

"What a wonderful memory. Did you ever talk with him after that?"

"Only a couple of times. He called me once to wish me a happy birthday."

"Wow, he was really the great communicator, wasn't he?" she asked.

"You bet. He gave all of us such a strong feeling that he believed in the greatness of our country and that we had a true patriot at the helm."

They paused to remember what it was like to have President Reagan in charge.

"Are you ready to make the wake-up call?" she asked.

Chapter 54

The altimeter was holding nicely. The altitude read out was still over twenty five thousand feet as he marked a half hour since separation. If this performance holds, he will have to descend at a higher rate than planned. No problem, just a recalculation and an adjustment. He would not make the final adjustment in the rate of descent until the last half hour of the planned flight. Twenty one thousand now. The darkest part of the night. He yawned and stretched, and took another swig of Gatorade.

Time for another report. They had agreed that he would hold the key down on his mike on a certain frequency for five seconds every half hour or so to indicate that all was normal. He held the key down and counted to five, then released it. Twenty thousand feet now.

The winds aloft had shifted in the last twenty minutes. He was drifting north of the course line, so he adjusted five degrees left on his heading. His little sailplane was a cocoon of silence. They hissed along together in the night.

He was grateful that it was a clear starry night, with a crescent moon. It would have been very challenging to have flown this flight in instrument conditions. Night flight is very challenging, nevertheless, and he missed seeing lights on the ground to give him perspective. As far as he could see in any direction, there was not a single light on the ground. The GPS indicated that he was about a hundred miles inside Iran, level now at eighteen thousand feet. The adjusted the true airspeed indicator for the new altitude.

Time for another report. He held the key down for a count of five and released it. There was complete silence in his earphones. The terrain below was hilly now and he looked forward to arriving over the central desert where it would be more hospitable for a landing.

The night passed more quickly than he thought it would. Perhaps the tension of flying over hostile territory enhanced the passage of time. Ahead, as far as he could see, the terrain began to smooth out. There was a subtle change in the appearance, too, with the color changing from a gray brown to a more brownish and tan color. It was still late in the night, but the moonlight enhanced the visibility of the ground for him.

He noticed that there had been another shift in the wind. He was now drifting south of the course line on the GPS. He corrected by turning to the right about three degrees. The ground speed readout on the GPS indicated that the wind was weaker now, but still a quartering tail wind. His ground speed was one hundred and eighty three miles per hour. This meant that he would reach the test site earlier than predicted and that he had enough altitude remaining that he could circle the area once to look for a place to land, rather than just barge in and land at the first relatively flat field he saw in the vicinity.

Chapter 55

The altitude now was sixteen thousand with eighty miles to go. He held the descent rate at one hundred fifty feet per minute. Over to his right, about eight miles from his position, he could see a light, just one light. Probably a village in the hills of eastern Iran. No other lights were visible. He looked back over his shoulder toward the southeast. The first glow of dawn was causing the blue-black sky to lighten a shade. He calculated that he would arrive over the test site before dawn, but it might be at the beginning of morning twilight. He took another swig of Gatorade.

Now the terrain below was definitely different. The sandy soil of the central desert was clearly a different shade than the foothills to the east. The altimeter read fourteen thousand three hundred. The course line looked good. He estimated another twenty minutes to the test site. The terrain at the test site was in the four thousand foot range, so he was holding alitiude well and was thankful for the accompanying tail winds. Without them, it would have been a real sweat to get this far at this altitude.

Time for another report, so he held the key down for five seconds again. Still no sound in his earphones. Now, it was just forty five miles to the test site. He would be over it in about twenty minutes. He hitched up in the seat and became more oriented to the appearance of the terrain below. He looked for a landmark to check his chart and GPS. He knew that the GPS was the ultimate authority, though. It was correct to a few feet and could be relied on completely.

As he looked from his left to his right, he saw nothing that might show up on the chart he held. He noticed on the chart that there was a line of hills, of moderate height, that would be across his line of flight on a north east to southwest orientation and he squinted ahead to see if he could see them. No joy. The altitude now was thirteen thousand two hundred. He corrected the airspeed indicator for that altitude and set it even lower for twelve five. As he finished that, he looked up and saw the line of hills that he had looked for and not seen just five minutes ago. Twenty five miles to the test site now.

There was definitely a lightening of the sky now. He had passed through the darkest of the night and dawn was only an hour or so away. He looked again and could not see a single house, power line, road or other vestige of man on the brown surface below. The altimeter now read eleven thousand eight hundred. Twenty miles to go. Time to get serious about finding a place to set down. The GPS course line was on the money, so he used that to check his chart again for a landing site. Ahead, about seven miles, he estimated, was another ridge of hills, higher this time, but still northeast to southwest oriented. Once over those hills, he would need to be looking for a landing site. The mine where the test was thought to be about to take place would be on the far slope of the next to the highest hill in his sight. He was pleased that he was arriving in the area right on course. His altimeter read eleven thousand three hundred.

As he passed over the line of hills, he confirmed that there was a nice sized open area to his left or southwest of the test site. It looked to be about two miles from the mine, at the closest edge, so he decided to circle over it to check it out closer. He did not have the luxury of picking a landing spot that was as good as a normal runway. Any place he could set down and survive the landing would be alright, but he wanted to land rather than crash, so he looked diligently.

On the southwest edge of the open area, there was what looked like an area that would be long enough and smooth enough for him. The hills to the east of it were plenty far enough to clear. He keyed the mike for five seconds. He thought it would be his last check in before landing. Still no sound in the earphones. He decided the area was good enough and flew over it from east to west. He had plenty of altitude, so he circled down. There was a small rise to the southwest of the landing zone, so he planned to come in over that, then deploy the spoilers to slow down and land. He entered a downwind leg for his chosen landing area and took another look out the side of the canopy as they went past. It looked a bit bumpier than he had thought, but he resolved to land there since damage to the aircraft was not a worry.

Now, he turned to the base leg perpendicular to the line of where he intended to land. The altimeter read five thousand one hundred, about a thousand feet above the terrain, he suspected. He deployed the spoilers earlier than he had planned, so he could make the final approach and get down to the field.

The hills that he had seen from above looked much larger when he was down to only about eight hundred feet above them. They were rocky and there did not seem to be any vegetation within sight.

The hills filled his field of view, now. He was committed to land. As they swept over the peak of the hills, the landing area appeared ahead. As he got down to about two hundred feet above the terrain, he noticed that is was rockier than he had observed. The rocks were the same color as the sandy soil, but he was committed and flew on. Now he was a hundred feet above the terrain. The rocks ahead were smaller and more dispersed. He found a sandy area almost straight ahead and touched down in a small shower of sand. As he rolled along, a two foot high rock to his right caught the right wing and spun them around. He felt a strong jolt and came to a halt sideways in a shower of dust. He was completely enveloped by the dust cloud and it took several seconds before it cleared enough for him to see. He immediately popped the canopy latch and began to get out. He had been strapped in for two and a half hours and he was stiff getting out, but he managed and sat down on a rock to the left of the nose. He counted himself lucky to have made it in with no injury. The sailplanes fuselage was broken about two feet in front of the empennage (tail) and the right wing was stove in, but not entirely broken off. He was banged up but had not fractures or cuts.

As he stood looking at the sailplane, a pang shot through him as he thought that he would soon be required to destroy this thing of beauty that had served him so well.

Chapter 56

No time for sentimentality. He went to the cockpit and began to put things into the rucksack. In ten minutes, he had it packed and was ready to get going. He would need to find a "hide" during the remainder of twilight and be secure before it got very light.

He turned on his hand held GPS. It took a full minute to boot up, but arrived at his location correctly. With great reluctance he armed the thermite charge and sat it in the pilot's seat of the sailplane. He left his helmet and the gear that he would not need again. Then he solemnly closed the canopy. He took a moment to say a prayer for the little sail plane and for a safe landing. In an hour, as soon as it was daylight, so the flames would not give away its position, the thermite charge would incinerate the beautiful sailplane.

He decided to go toward the hills to the west of his position and try to get a position on the east slope where he could see the mine entrance. He looked back one last time at the sailplane and said a prayer of thanksgiving for it, the people who designed and built it, the men who helped get it to him and the guys in the cab at Creech and Bagram who guided the MQ-9 to tow him aloft.

It took Lero an hour and a half to make his way across the up sloping terrain to the peak of the ridge opposite the mine entrance. He found a large boulder at the peak with a cleft behind it that would afford enough shelter. He put his rucksack in the cleft and got out the items he thought he might need: the special hand held transceiver with the aiming device and emission aiming device, handgun, radar reflector, binoculars, and an MRE. He had not eaten since the afternoon before. He swigged some Gatorade and sat down to eat the MRE.

The special transceiver had a tube attached to it that was lined with thin lead foil to shield the transmissions and allow them to only exit the tube in the direction in which the tube was pointed. He consulted his hand held GPS and wrote down the coordinates.

It was now morning twilight and the sun would be coming up in about half an hour. He could see across the valley to the mine entrance about two miles away. Using the binoculars, he scanned the area. There were no personnel outside the mine entrance. Everyone in Dr. Abbasi's party evidently were inside.

Before he sent his first message, he got out and checked the laser designator. The battery back did its job and the test circuit indicated "ready," so he powered it off and put in on the front side of the cleft, while he readied the transceiver.

He had not spoken in some time and his voice startled him as he spoke into the transceiver. "Jolly Roger, Jolly Roger, this is Blackbeard. Position is approximately two miles west of the site. Good visibility. Good shelter. Systems checked okay. Ready when you are."

"Blackbeard, this is Jolly Roger. Report received and understood. Stand by."

"What do we do now?" asked Jean.

"Ask him how he would advise we proceed. Do we need both kinds of missile?" asked Ernie.

Jean keyed the mike. "Blackbeard, this is Jolly Roger. Advise how to proceed."

As Lero heard Jean's voice, a shower of feelings swept over him. It was so good to hear her voice, even if she were eight thousand miles away. She was experiencing the same kind of feelings on her end.

He aimed the transceiver and keyed the mike, "Advise firecracker first. Hold the alternative for possible second swat. Advise when ready."

"No time like the present. Go ahead. Advise when one hundred clicks out, so I can use the magic wand."

"Understood. Under way shortly. Will report."

Lero knew that very soon, Module Eighteen would fulfill its purpose for the first time. He wondered what it was like for Jean and Ernie to actually fire it up.

"Okay," said Ernie, "Time to get with the program. Read me the next step in the launch protocol."

"The next step is to choose a missile," said Jean. "Which one do we want?"

"Well, since Lero wants to try a high explosive missile first, we will use Missile number Three. Since the flight time is approximately sixty three minutes, we should go ahead and launch once it is ready."

"How long after we choose Number Three, will it be ready?"

"We believe, since we have never tested it before, that it will take about a minute and a half for the missile to be readied for launch. Each missile is launched from its own tube. The onboard computer runs a check of its systems and indicates ready by a two letter signal. Listen for it."

The sat in silence while the Module did its checks.

Jean heard a clear signal in her earphones. "D" and "W."

"It is ready. Did you hear the signal?" she asked.

Ernie nodded.

"What is the launch code for Missile Three?" she asked.

"It is a five letter message. I will read it to you. Copy it down to be sure to send it correctly. "Papa, Alpha, Golf, Mike, Sierra. Send those letters and it will launch in approximately thirty seconds. It will confirm a launch with a three letter code. Add ten seconds back to the three letter code to get the true launch time for calculations. Go ahead."

Jean steadied herself for a couple of seconds before she typed: "P, A, G, M, S."

They waited to hear the confirmation of launch message.

In a few seconds, as they watched their digital clock, came the message, "V, E, K."

Jean wrote down the hour, minutes and seconds. She keyed her satellite phone. Lero answered on the second ring.

"Fat is in the fire," she said.

"Understood. Advise five minutes out." The line went silent.

Now all they had to do was wait. Lero had marked his watch for the time of her call and estimated sixty three minutes after that. He wrote the time down on his small clip board and crawled up to the edge to have another look. The valley was deserted, not a human trace in sight. Two thousand pounds of high explosive was hurtling toward him and the valley at twenty five thousand miles an hour. It as an eerie feeling. He put down the binoculars and crawled back into the cleft behind the boulder.

He got out the laser designator and once again pressed the power button. The green LED came on by the handle. He instructed it digitally to do a systems check. It checked OK. He turned it off and lay back to wait. It was going to be a long hour in some ways and a short hour in other ways. He thought of Jean.

Chapter 57

The hours passed quickly. No one had appeared in his night vision goggles or his binoculars at or near the mine. He noticed that he was sweating all over even though it was a cool dawn. The earpiece connected to Lero's handheld transceiver crackled faintly and a female voice said, "Five minutes. Acknowledge."

He keyed the mike circuit and broadcast. "Acknowledge. Five minutes." He looked at his watch and marked the time. He waited a couple of minutes, then crawled up to the top of the ridge next to the boulder. He wondered what it would look like in five minutes as he gazed across the valley.

There was no activity at the mine entrance, no lights or movement. Time seemed to accelerate. At two minutes to go, he pointed the laser designator at the mine entrance and pressed the grip trigger. He could see the light splashing on the mine entrance area in his night vision goggles. He did not waver. He held on it. Then, came a loud swooshing sound. The missile hit at about a seventy degree down angle just to the left of the center of the entrance. There was an immediate huge ball of fire and

Lero ducked behind the slope of the hill to shield himself from the blast. The ground shook and the fireball lit up the night. There was a tremendous sound when it reached him. He had held his hands over his ears for protection, but the sound was so loud that he felt it in his bones. Small rocks shook loose from the slope and rolled down beside him. After the jolt of the blast, he gathered up his gear and went back up to the edge for one more look. The mountain side where the entrance had been looked very different. It reminded him of the before and after pictures of Mount Saint Helens. The slope was different and there was a large cloud of dust from the displaced rock and dirt that had formed the new side of the mountain. The sky was still lit up by the fireball above the blast site. He might as well have been looking at a moonscape.

Chapter 58

"Do you have instructions about when to conduct the test," asked Ferrydoon.

"No, the Supreme Leader put in our hands to make that decision. I think we should proceed without hesitation. Let's eat and rest a bit, then we can take a golf cart farther into the mine where the device is located and proceed to input the instructions to conduct the test. The plan is for us to withdraw to a safe distance while we await the test. If, for some reason, the device fails, you and I will return to it to determine what went wrong, so we can make any changes needed in the design of the trigger for another attempt and we can salvage the fissile materials so they can be reformed if necessary."

After they had rested, they climbed into a golf cart and made the trip about a quarter mile back into the mine, to where they had previously placed the device. For security reasons, they were the only persons allowed past a certain checkpoint in the mine. All told, there were only twelve persons in the mine, all of whom had highest security clearances.

Dr.Ferrydoon stopped the golf cart about fifty feet from the device. They had previously set up battery powered flood lights and he went over and turned them on before turning off the lights on the golf cart.

Abbasi had his heavy leather brief case with him. As the approached the device, he gently swung the briefcase up onto a table that they had set up. In the briefcase was a three inch thick notebook that contained the protocols for arming the device and conducting the test.

Dr. Abbasi and Dr. Ferrydoon began by checking the installation of the trigger after it had been placed where they would conduct the test. Then they began to follow the notebook's protocol for the test. After Dr. Abbasi would read an instruction or challenge from the procedure, Dr. Ferrydoon would reply. They were about halfway through the list when, for no particular reason, Dr. Ferrydoon looked up past Dr. Abbasi and saw a wall of flame coming at them at blinding speed. It was his last thought.

Chapter 59

True to the plan, he strapped his rucksack closed and slung it over his shoulder and started down the slope to the west. He had been walking down the dusty slope for about two minutes when the earth moved beneath him. He lost his footing and sat down hard. The earth shuddered and rocks were set loose on the slope to roll down beside him and below him. He looked quickly up the slope to see if any rocks were coming down toward him, but saw none. The tremor continued for about twenty seconds. The earth seemed to move side to side and up and down alternately. Since he had nothing to hold onto, he lay down and spread his arms and legs to keep from rolling down the slope. The tremor gradually subsided and in about two minutes, the earth was calm again. There were deep sounds all around him, but no more tremors.

He got to his feet and walked down the slope away from the direction of the mine entrance. He crossed a narrow valley and went up the slope of the next hill to the crest. When he got there, he could see most of the side of the mountain where the mine had been, now about three miles away, but he could not see low enough on the mountain to see the exact spot where the mine had been. The slope had changed again, this time more sunken than before. There were areas on the slope where dust clouds still marked the avalanches caused by the second tremor.

He took several pictures with his smartphone and put it in his pocket. Then he took out a Gatorade and his compass. He swigged a nice gulp of the Gatorade and looked at the compass. He reckoned west was best, and started walking. After about forty minutes, the rucksack became very heavy and he decided to look for a place to hide. There was a clump of boulders on the upslope ahead of him and when he got there, he found a nice hidey hole near the center of the boulders. He laid down on the rucksack and fell asleep quickly.

Chapter 60

"Holy Cow," said Ernie. The U. S. Geological Survey is reporting two tremors in that vicinity, one about one point eight on the Richter Scale and the second about four point two. The explosive must have caused the device to detonate. Holy Cow."

He keyed his computer to the USGS site and waited. The warning symbol appeared and a note below it said, "Two tremors in central Iran. Possible earthquake. Largest measures 4.2."

"I was ready to launch the nuclear missile, but I am relieved and glad we don't have to," said Ernie. "It would have been unprecedented and scary. Another benefit is that we know that Module Eighteen works and also we still have all the nukes in case we ever need them."

Jean was still in a state over the explosions. She was worried about Lero since they had not heard from him since the missile strike. It was an agonizing wait.

Lero awoke, and checked his watch and saw that he had been asleep for two hours and a half. He carefully checked the area for movement and saw none. He took reached for his satellite phone which was on a lanyard on his left wrist, but when he pulled it up to use it, he saw that a rock had landed on it during the aftershock and it was now useless. All he had to communicate with now was his hand held air band transceiver.

Jean and Ernie had not heard from Lero since the two events. They watched and waited, but no broadcast came.

Lero reckoned that he was about four miles (or seven kilometers,or clicks) from the mine entrance. There was very little shelter other than the boulders where he hid. He decided to stay there and rest a little in case there might be a patrol nearby.

Chapter 61

"This is Fox News. The British Broadcasting Corporation is reporting that the government of The Islamic Republic of Iran has reported that a large meteorite struck the earth in remote central Iran. The exact location is nearly fifty miles east of the village of Sedi Karak, which is about four hundred miles southeast of Tehran. Authorities are guarded about the number of casualties, but observers in the village of Sedi Karak reported a large flash and a massive explosion followed by a large dust cloud which was raised by the impact. Seismographs around the world recorded two tremors: a smaller one and then a larger one measuring four point two on the Richter scale. The Red Crescent has rushed aid to the area, but is still struggling to access the site which is quite remote. Stay tuned to Fox News for updates on this unusual, but large meteor strike."

Jean and Ernie looked at each other without expression.

In a few minutes, the satellite telephone rang. It was Colonel Haskins at CentCom, with a report.

"Just wanted to bring you up to date," he said to Ernie. "Lero was painting with a laser designator just before the 'meteor" struck. He said he was about two miles from the site. We have not heard from him since. We will let you know immediately when we have any news."

"I understand, Colonel. Thank you for calling personally. We will stand by. Thank you," said Jean.

Chapter 62

Sergeant Major Hopkins was sleeping next to the duty desk at Forward Operating Base Kilo Thirteen when the call came in.

"This is Colonel Myers at CentCom. Can you paint a helicopter white and put a red crescent on it and fly it into Iran to pick up some survivors of the meteor strike?"

"Colonel, I will have to check to see if we have enough white paint to do that. I will advise as soon as I can."

"Very well. Sooner the better, Sergeant Major. We will have coordinates for the pickup of survivors for you when you report."

"Good night! We cannot fly a helicopter that far into Iran and back without refueling. How are we going to get fuel out there to those guys?" he thought to himself.

He dialed the number for his helicopter crew chief, Sergeant Goodall. He answered on the first ring.

"Goodall, can you fly a helicopter about two hundred miles into Iran with a fuel blivit with enough fuel in it to refuel another helicopter and your own helicopter and get back to base?"

"Sergeant Major, if we strip out all the armament and only fill the blivit with enough fuel for the mission, I think we can do it. The crew would have to be limited to the two pilots and one crew member, though."

"How soon can you be ready to leave?"

"It will take a couple of hours to load the blivit and fill it with the right amount of fuel. What about insignia, Sergeant Major?"

"Orders are to paint the helicopter white with a Red Crescent insignia. Do you think the crew can paint a helo that fast?"

"If we just spray it and don't spend any time making it neat or preparing the surface, we can do that in about two hours."

"Good. Get on it then. Pick your crew and have them report to me for a briefing."

"Will do," said Sergeant Goodall and picked up a clip board and left the tent.

Chapter 63

Lero had been waiting and watching for over three hours before he heard the sound of a distant helicopter. He was growing more and more apprehensive about a patrol in the area. In a little while, it came near, but on the other side of the ridge from his hiding place and he could not see it, nor determine which direction it was from him, nor what direction it was going.

In about an hour, he thought he heard another distant helicopter. It was to his west and out of sight over the ridge behind him. He scrambled up to the peak and looked over. The valley beyond him was more of the same terrain. No vegetation to speak of and a broad, low valley between him and the next peak. He could see the helicopter about three miles away to his southwest. It was a Russian MI-9 and painted white. He could see and hear the helicopter coming back in his direction, so he got out his hand held transceiver.

As he turned it to the international emergency frequency, one twenty one decimal five kilohertz, he heard: "Red Rover, Red Rover, this is Silver Bullet. Do you copy?"

Lero turned the broadcast power down to a low level so as not to reach out too far to avoid detection and keyed his transceiver. "Silver Bullet, this is Red Rover. I have you in sight. I am on the ridge to your northeast, about three miles, near a large boulder. I will step out into the clear when you get close."

"Roger, Red Rover. We will approach. Looking for you."

The helicopter had to make a couple of course corrections to get near to him, but when it was about two hundred yards from the peak of the ridge, Lero stepped out from behind the boulder and waved to them. The helo came over top of him, trailing a harness that they had lowered in anticipation. They came and hovered over him about fifty feet above the sloping terrain. The dust cloud was dense under the downwash of the heavy helicopter and the sand and small gravel stung his face. They lowered a harness on a cable and it came down the slope toward him. He grabbed it and, in a moment, attached his rucksack to the carabiner and he got into the harness and began to be winched up to the waiting open hatch. The helo started back east as soon as he was in the harness and clear of terrain. He was inside before they got halfway across the valley. As they swept out of the valley, he got a last look at the vicinity where the mine entrance had been. He formed the impression of a large area of devastation, that if there had been any trees in the area, they would have been blown down by the explosion. He turned in his seat to the bulkhead and sobbed with relief and exhaustion. It was such a relief to think of going back to Jean.

Chapter 64

Ernie knocked on the door jamb of the darkened room. Across the room, Jean stirred in her bunk and raised up on one elbow. He was silhouetted in the door opening.

"What's up?" she asked, groggily..

"Just got a call from CentCom. Our guy was picked up about an hour ago by our special operations guys in a Russian helo painted with Red Crescent insignia. They are departing Iran to the east and will go to Forward Operating Base Kilo Thirteen about a hundred miles west of Kandahar. They said they would call when our guys are back to the base."

"Thank God, Ernie. Thank you for coming to tell me. Let me know if you hear any more."

"I will, Jean. You get some rest."

Jean's eyes were full of tears, but she had a smile on her face as she turned once more to her pillow.

Chapter 65

Ernie went back to his laboratory to watch for developments. He had his television tuned to the BBC channel, at the moment.

As he browsed the settings of the console in front of him and made log entries, the lady announcer on the television said, "This is BBC News London. The communications office of the Islamic Republic of Iran announced today that a large meteor struck the ground in the central desert in their country about four hundred miles southeast of Tehran. It was believed that there were no human casualties, however, some livestock were killed by the resulting explosion and devastation. Seismographs in surrounding countries recorded the tremor caused by the impact. It was calculated by observers to be the equivalent to an earthquake with a measurement of four point one on the Richter scale. The Islamic Republic said a more thorough report will be forthcoming when investigators get to the site with testing equipment and cameras. Stay tuned to BBC for ongoing coverage of the meteor strike."

Ernie turned back to his console and made an entry into his log. Overhead, Module Eighteen dozed on, its Cesium battery good for another thirty years.

Chapter 66

By the time the helo got to Forward Operating Base Kilo Thirteen, the sun was setting behind them. The base was well camouflaged and they could not pick it out from the surrounding terrain until they were within two miles. The pilot set the MI-9 down softly in a huge cloud of dust, then began to go through his post flight shutdown, carefully monitoring the temperatures before actually shutting down the engines. The crew, on the other hand, exited immediately and helped Lero down to the steel mats that made up the helo landing area. He was weak in his legs and needed their help. One of them brought his rucksack to the waiting Suburban and in a couple of minutes, he was on his way to the base HQ.

Sergeant Major Hopkins greeted him as they pulled up and helped him into the tent where the command post was. He had taken the precaution of having a medical corpsman be there to attend to Lero. As they lowered Lero into a comfortable chair, the Sergeant Major stepped back to give the corpsman a chance to check Lero over. The first thing the corpsman did was to take Lero's pulse and blood pressure. Then he produced a flask of brandy and told Lero to take a healthy gulp. It was a welcome touch. Lero had been through quite a bit and was weary from the fatigue and stress. In a few minutes, he asked if he could lie down and sleep for a while and they took him to a bunk. The corpsman stayed by his bedside while he slept.

Chapter 67

Hopkins dialed his satellite telephone. "CentCom Ops Central, Major Brophy speaking."

"Major Brophy, this is Sergeant Major Hopkins at FOB Kilo Thirteen. Advise CentCom and Mr. Murfree that the man of the hour is safe in our care."

"Will do, Sergeant Major. Nice piece of work."

"My men are tops, sir. I just sit and watch," said Hopkins.

"I know better than that, Sergeant Major. Congratulations. Get some rest."

"Roger, sir. Good evening."

They hung up.

Chapter 68

When Lero awakened, the first think he asked for was a satellite telephone. As he sat wearily on the side of the bed, an aide brought him the phone. He dialed a familiar number. On the third ring, Jean answered.

"Hello," she said. Lero was so overcome, he could not speak. She knew it was him and she sobbed. It was more than a minute before either of them could speak. Finally he said, "This is your blue eyed beauty. I will be home soon. Don't worry, I am fine. As soon as possible I will come home."

"I am so relieved. So happy. Ernie sends his congratulations. We are so relieved that you are not hurt. You have been through so much. Come home," she said.

 "I will. See you soon. I love you," he sobbed.

She sobbed, too, as she said, "I love you, too."

They hung up.

Chapter 69

When the Suburban pulled up to the South Portico, President Thompson and Janice were waiting to greet Lero and Jean. It was a warm and wonderful moment. They went in and had a nice private visit and dinner in the residence.

As dessert was served, President Thompson said, "Our reports indicate that the first blast actually triggered the second. It was calculated that the device was the equivalent to a forty thousand tons. The unfortunate event will, undoubtedly set their progress back quite a few months and may deter them longer than that. Protocol prevents me from contacting Ernie, so I want you to assure him that we are supremely grateful to him for all of his past work and for helping you and Jean accomplish your mission. After we were told you were safe, we both thanked the Lord that you were not injured and would be coming home soon. I cast about for some way to repay you for what you have done for your country, but, under the circumstances, the only thing I can offer is our profound thanks and to ask you to continue to head up the unit at Davis Monthan. Could you see your way clear to do that?"

"Sir, it has been a great honor to serve in the unit. I will be glad to do so. May I keep my present staff?" he asked gesturing with his head toward Jean.

"Of course," said the President. "Janice and I wish you both the very best. Thank you again."

They slept in the White House that night and had a fine breakfast with President Thompson and the First Lady before leaving the same way they came, in an anonymous black Suburban. A Grumman Gulfstream V was sitting at Stevens Aviation for them when they arrived at Reagan National Airport. The co-pilot greeted them in the pilot's lounge and said that the President was sending her crew west anyway and they "just happened" to have room to take them to Tucson. It was one of those beautiful, clear blue days. The G-V departed Runway Three six and made a quick left turn to avoid the Washington Monument and the Prohibited Area that covered the White House. Jean and Lero held hands all the way back to Tucson, with other occasional exchanges of affection.